I0669871

THE WAR BUSINESS

SAM RAVEN
BOOK FOUR

BRIAN DRAKE

ROUGH
EDGES
PRESS

The War Business
Paperback Edition
Copyright © 2025 (As Revised) Brian Drake

Rough Edges Press
An Imprint of Wolfpack Publishing
1707 E. Diana Street
Tampa, FL 33610

roughedgespress.com

Paperback ISBN 978-1-68549-398-1
Ebook ISBN 978-1-68549-397-4

This fourth Sam Raven adventure is dedicated to our cat, Buster, who walks across my keyboard in an effort to improve my books (it's actually his way of guaranteeing my attention when he wants food). So far has only managed to type lines like:

xcsgdhyrfutgikhojkiutrdkvgyublfjnioegtbkdmh;
Wegfdftyrt678iolkjhgtr5678;
and
ghjk987654edfghjcvbhytre34567890plkjhgfds.

Sometimes he hits an unknown combination resulting in my laptop freezing haha. Always back up your work!

Of course, looking at the example above, he might be onto something...

THE WAR BUSINESS

SAM RAVEN STIFLED A GRUNT AND ARCHED HIS BACK. THE ROPE binding his wrists tightened. The woman behind him laughed. She was having way too much fun.

"Does it hurt?" the woman said. "I'd hate to think I'm losing my touch."

"Feels like a massage." Raven gritted his teeth. "I actually have an itch on my back. Since you're in the neighborhood?" She jerked the ropes again and Raven groaned audibly.

"Think you're funny?"

"I'm hilarious," he said.

"Your imaginary friends agree."

"They're not all bad, you know."

The top edge of the chair dug into his back and made sitting without squirming difficult. He fought the urge to shift. Nothing would make him comfortable for the time being. The strain in his right shoulder and upper back grew with each passing second.

Zenya had tied the rope well.

"Tight as I could make it," the Russian woman said as she

stepped in front of Raven. "You should feel numb in a few minutes."

"Can't wait." Raven tugged once for show and tugged again to see exactly how screwed he was. He was strapped like a mattress in the bed of a pickup. He wasn't going anywhere.

Great.

The only other man in the room watched from the corner. Zenya looked at the other man. He left the corner and joined her.

They made an odd pair in the low light of the storage room. The bulb over Raven's head shined bright, highlighting them as well as the boxes of booze stacked in the room.

The man said, "You have interfered with our plans for the last time, Mr. Raven."

"You can kill me right now," Raven said, "if you're going to throw B-movie lines at me. I expected more from you, Yuri."

"How I tell you we are done with you is my business." The stocky Russian, shorter than the woman beside him, thumped his broad chest. He dyed his hair black but forgot about his mustache; it showed flecks of gray.

"Those diamonds do not belong to you," Raven said.

"You are as much a mercenary as I. You want them for yourself."

"No, the family you stole from hired me to get the diamonds back."

"And since you have failed, they lose the diamonds and the cash they paid you. Isn't Mr. Raven unlucky, Zenya?"

"Total jinx. He's an idiot. A moron. A complete and useless—"

"You've made your point, my darling," the stocky Russian said. He turned back to Raven. "And you. You made a mistake trying to get me at my bar. We spotted you as soon as you walked through the door."

Raven grimaced again. His aches were turning to dull throbs. "No plan is perfect." He tried to shift his right arm but the rope only bit into his skin.

"I know my knots, Mr. Raven." Zenya smiled. "I'm an expert. When I tie a man, he doesn't get out. He's totally at my mercy. Still having a good time?"

Raven felt sweat on his forehead. If he was walking out alive, he'd need to depend on previous arrangements. He glanced again at Zenya and began to doubt those arrangements still existed. If she wanted the diamonds for herself...

The tall red-headed woman wore a blouse and skirt combo and stood with her hands on her hips. The pose was a sure-fire way to attract the attention of any healthy male. She even had an effect on Raven. But her face showed contempt. Her dark eyes examined him as if he were a lab rat. Tied to the chair, he felt like a *trapped* rat. Maybe she'd feed him a piece of cheese if he asked nicely.

"Do I get to hurt him now, Yuri?" she said.

"By all means, my darling."

"First," Zenya said, "I'm going to slice off your eyelids." She bent over to put her face close to Raven's. "Then I am going to slice off your cheeks. After that—"

"Kill me by talking too much? Damn, Zenya, between Yuri's bad movie lines and your motor mouth I wish you'd have shot me two days ago."

Yuri Panov laughed. "I wish too."

Zenya slapped Raven. His face jerked to the right and the sting on his face made him forget the ache in his back.

"Then I will slice off your lips," Zenya continued, "so you can no longer talk back like a naughty boy."

"Promise?"

Another slap. Raven didn't fight the low moan pushing up

from his belly. He let his head hang down. *Think of something fast, Sammy.*

"Look at me, Mr. Raven."

Raven raised bleary eyes at the redhead.

"Want to guess where I hide my knife?"

"Obviously not in your cheeks."

"Ha! Guess again."

"The same place you asked me to stick—"

"*Nyet!*" She raised a finger in warning. "I will show you." Zenya grabbed a handful of her skirt, both hands at her waist. She dug her fingers into the fabric and pulled the hem up along her stockinged legs.

Raven watched the hem rise. He cleared his throat. "Torture mixed with a striptease would be great on the internet. Ever consider an OnlyFans account?"

"You have made your last joke, Mr. Raven." Zenya stopped, holding her skirt up with one hand. With her left she reached for the exposed garter belt on her right thigh. The strap doubled as a sheath for a shiny stiletto. She drew the knife, let the skirt fall back into place, and transferred the stiletto to her right hand.

"Say goodbye to your eyelids, Mr. Raven."

Zenya took a step forward.

Raven tried to swallow but his throat was dry.

Yuri Panov made a nervous squeak. Zenya glared at him.

"You must excuse me, my darling. I am a humble jewel thief, not a murderer. The sight of blood makes me nauseous. That's why I hire people to kill for me."

"Who said anything about murder?" she asked.

Yuri started for the door. "Please keep the mess to a minimum, my darling."

He opened the door and went out. The door clicked shut. Raven and Zenya locked eyes.

"He's gone?" Raven said.

"You idiot. You stupid, stupid—"

"Stop talking and cut me loose."

She moved to the back of the chair. She sliced several times and the rope dropped away. Raven rubbed his arms and moved his right shoulder.

"You weren't supposed to do this tonight," she said.

"Spur of the moment."

"You're lucky I was here."

"For a moment I thought you forgot our deal."

"Never." She smiled and reached up her skirt again. From her left thigh she pulled a compact nine-millimeter pistol. She handed the gun to Raven. It was warm from being close to her skin.

"What else do you hide up there?" he said.

She grinned. "Maybe you'll find out in Paris."

Raven checked the gun. A bullet sat in the chamber, ready to fire. "Don't be late."

"Don't forget to show up."

"Never."

Raven started for the door.

"Hey."

He turned.

"You should scream. Make it look good."

"Nuts," Raven said. "They'll think you're still talking."

As her face flushed red, he opened the door and exited the storage room.

2

PANOV'S BAR WASN'T LARGE. LONG BAR ON ONE SIDE. SHELVES full of bottles, most in various stages of fullness. The glass reflected the bright overhead lights with the aid of a long mirror. Hardwood floor polished smooth. Tables opposite the bar. Any "private business", the sole purpose of the bar, happened in either of the two rooms next to the storage room.

Raven advanced down a short hallway with cautious steps. The two meeting rooms were on his right. They held no interest. The open doorway to the bar waited a few steps ahead. Panov was talking to somebody, a man named Gustav Kouralis. A killer from Greece. The man Panov paid to do the dirty work he said made him nauseous.

Kouralis had taken Raven's pistol when they'd hauled him into the back. Raven wanted his gun. The small pistol Zenya provided would hopefully do the trick. Raven swung through the doorway.

Panov and Kouralis, on either side of the bar, Panov holding a bottle, stopped talking. Kouralis let his glass fall. It shattered as he made a grab for the gun under his jacket.

Raven fired once. Kouralis caught the slug in the neck and his scream resembled a gargle. He slid off the stool but didn't fall. He staggered back as blood spilled down his neck to soak his shirt.

Raven shot Panov high in the chest, then shifted to fire at Kouralis again. The Greek fell dead. Raven slipped around the bar to where Panov thrashed on the floor. He made whining sounds coupled with pleading eyes and Raven shot him again and left him there.

Raven retrieved his Nighthawk Custom .45 autoloader from the Greek killer's belt. When he turned, Zenya stood in the doorway watching with eager eyes.

"Are they dead?"

"Yes. Where are the sparklies?"

Zenya motioned for him to follow. She led him to an office at the end of the hall. Panov's cluttered desk sat inside. The room wasn't big enough for the two of them so from the doorway she told Raven where to find the briefcase. Panov stored it in a hidden drawer under his desk. Raven removed the case from the hidden compartment, placed it on top, and raised the lid. The diamond necklace sat in an interior pocket. Raven held the necklace in his hand for a moment. The shimmering diamonds had a nice weight to them.

"Isn't it pretty?"

He shook his head and put the necklace back. Closing the case, he said, "It doesn't belong to you either."

She pouted. "You're no fun. You'll be boring in Paris."

"Thank you for not lying to me."

"I told you. No need to accuse me—"

"Zenya, for heaven's sake, shut up."

She folded her arms and looked mad.

Raven held the case in his left hand. "Better scoot. Your gun was a little loud."

"Speaking of my gun—"

"You may have it back in Paris. Move your butt."

"Yes, master," she said. With a wink and lick of her lips, Zenya took off. Raven waited till he heard the back door shut.

Then he placed Zenya's gun on the desk and exited out the back as well.

Nobody ambushed him from the shadows.

THE CAPER STARTED in London with the theft of an heirloom from an old money family. Their oldest daughter, celebrating her 21st birthday, was the latest in the line to enjoy a long tradition. Her grandmother passed down the necklace she'd received on her 21st birthday. The necklace was worth millions and had been passed down to the oldest daughters for three generations. The young woman's happiness lasted the evening; by morning, the necklace had vanished, and joy turned to sorrow.

Scotland Yard identified Russian jewel thief Yuri Panov as the culprit right away. He'd attended the party under an alias and posed as a rich Russian oligarch moving through social circles in the United Kingdom. When the Yard lost track of Panov, the family reached out to Sam Raven.

Raven's underworld contacts said he might find Panov at his bar in Moscow. Raven traveled to Russia, where he bumped into Zenya Oromatova. She was a noted jewel aficionado (i.e., thief) who planned to steal the necklace from Panov.

Raven knew Zenya from two previous adventures. He knew how her mind worked. He proposed a deal. Help him get to Panov, and he'd split his $250,000 fee. He'd also split the promised million-dollar bonus for recovering the necklace. Zenya agreed. She was only interested in cash. Nicking jewels from rich families was the best way she knew how to keep her accounts full. Why get a real job?

Zenya worked her way into Panov's confidence as a buyer for the necklace, and Raven did the rest. Albeit not as stealthily as planned. Luckily, Zenya kept up her part of the bargain.

Raven returned the necklace to the happy family and confirmed the transfer of funds. With a date in Paris, he didn't stay long in London, but hopped a flight to Paris. Upon arriving, Raven checked in at his favorite hotel, within walking distance of the Eiffel Tower.

He kept to a routine while he waited for Zenya, having breakfast and lunch at the hotel's outdoor café. The locals and tourists gave him plenty to watch. The mix of languages became a game as he tried to identify which region of the world each tourist had come from. Except those who spoke English. He had an easy time picking out the Americans, Canadians and Brits.

Zenya arrived two days later.

"Hello, Sam."

She pulled out a chair and sat before Raven responded. She wore her hair tied back, faded jeans, blouse knotted above her belly button. No makeup. Perhaps she didn't want to drive the women of Paris to suicide by looking better than them.

Raven poured her a glass of wine from the half bottle on the table. He didn't like wine and had a beer in front of him, with the remains of his lunch on a plate he'd set aside.

"Figured you liked red," he said.

"You're not funny." She grabbed the glass before he finished pouring. Raven tipped the bottle upright to avoid a spill. He set the bottle down.

"White, then?"

"You tried to, how you say, jam me in."

"Jam you *up*, actually. And 'we' haven't used the phrase since the '30s. You've been watching American gangster movies, haven't you?"

Zenya leaned forward, elbows on the table, and Raven blinked. She looked mad enough to leap across the table and rip open his neck with her long nails. Which he noticed she'd painted red.

"You left my gun in Moscow."

"It would have been boring getting out of the city without the Moscow police on your tail."

"*Nyet*. It was easy. This is where you messed up. They can't trace the gun to me."

"Then why are you mad?"

"The gun was a gift. A very special gift."

"You don't strike me as the sentimental type."

She sat back and smiled, which brought a mischievous glint to her dark eyes. "First man I ever—you know." She slashed a finger across her throat. "He never saw my knife. He was so impressed that as he died, he gave me the gun."

"Fascinating. Bullshit, but fascinating."

"It is okay. You thought you were playing a joke. I take something from you next. Your locket, maybe?"

The silver chain, visible around his neck, ended at a scuffed sterling silver locket under his shirt. He never told anybody what it contained. He never looked himself. He knew what was in there. His conscience. The force motivating his war without end. The ghosts who urged him to fight for those without a champion.

Raven turned serious. "Touch it and I'll make you eat your fingers."

She laughed. "I like my fingers. I like doing things with my fingers."

"Counting money?"

"Speaking of money—"

"In my room."

"Cash?"

"Electronic transfer. Safer. I don't make a habit of walking around with a crap ton of cash."

"We will go to your room," she said, "after wine." She grabbed the bottle and filled her glass to the top.

RAVEN HAD Zenya half undressed before the hotel room door shut.

At least it seemed as such. He only had the knot of her blouse undone, and the sight of her pale white belly was enough to rev the engines. Two more buttons held the blouse together.

They breathed hard like animals unleashed from a cage. Zenya's wine-scented breath flooded his senses as he steered her to the bed. She knocked a foot out from under him and threw him onto the mattress. He landed on his back with a laugh.

Zenya straddled his legs at the knees and clawed at his belt. She pulled too hard moving the zipper down and Raven hoped she hadn't torn anything. The trousers hadn't been cheap.

"Now I will show you"—she tugged his pants down a little —"lift your ass, darling—what I like to do with my fingers."

Once she had Raven's pants and boxers off, she began her demonstration, narrating the effort.

3

LATER IN THE EVENING, RAVEN STOOD AT THE WINDOW looking out at nighttime Paris. Raven had never met a woman as insatiable as Zenya Oromatova. She was willing to do things even he found objectionable. But everybody runs out of gas and she was no exception. The Russian redhead lay on her stomach beneath a tangle of covers, snoring. Raven, restless, left the bed to stand naked in front of the window and looked out at the lights of Paris.

But not before snaking his locket off the nightstand and putting it back around his neck. He didn't think Zenya would try and take it; the locket was his only connection to his past life. He wore it to remember what anybody else would want to forget.

He'd been a CIA operative; before that, 82nd Airborne and Special Forces, eager to serve his country. When he'd had enough of fighting, he left active service to settle as a civilian. Then tragedy struck, and he went back to war. But not for his country this time. He went back to war to save others from the tragedy fate had dealt him. When protection wasn't possible, he avenged.

It was a lonely life broken by sporadic distraction like Zenya Oromatova, but such distractions were temporary. He had a feeling his time with her was ending, which was why he couldn't sleep. Something, or somebody, was out there, calling to him through the ether. He'd know for sure soon enough.

He wasn't aware Zenya had stopped snoring. Nor did he hear her rise. When she snaked warm arms around his torso, he jerked in surprise.

"If you're still awake, I haven't done a very good job," she said. "Why are you awake?"

"Couldn't sleep."

"There's something on your mind. Is it another woman? Are you cheating on her with me?"

"What if I said yes?"

"I'd say you're a naughty man and should be punished, but I didn't bring my paddle."

"I may have to leave soon."

"Not before you give me my money." She ran her fingers through the hair on his chest. He felt her soft breasts pressing into his back as she leaned against him.

"Where are you going?"

"I don't know."

"You are waiting for a ghost to give you directions?"

If you only knew. "Maybe."

She scratched her nails down his chest to his belly and then let her fingers travel further. He grunted as she seized him.

"What's happening down here?"

He turned, grabbed her below her bottom and lifted her off the floor. "You talk too much, Zenya." She let out a squeal of delight and he dropped her on the bed and moved on top of her. She opened her legs to accommodate him and he went in with an easy thrust and Zenya's eyes rolled back.

"You're right…oh…oh…less…ahhhhh…talking…oh my…
more…oh, yes, don't stop."

He didn't.

RAVEN TRANSFERRED her money as promised the next
morning. She joked about feeling sore. He said if she could
still walk, he hadn't done a very good job. And then Zenya
Oromatova went her own way. It was a simple goodbye with
no promises about seeing each other again. But Raven knew
it wasn't the last time he'd see the crazy Russian redhead.
Their paths would cross again. Someday.

He stayed in Paris for lack of anywhere else to go at the
moment. He was waiting for the call, the cry for help, whatever it was alerting him to more action in the war without
end. Paris was as good a place as any to receive the message.

Meanwhile, he might as well enjoy the wait. During lunch
he thought about a CIA pal he hadn't seen in a few years
named Aaron Osborne. They'd served together in Iraq, part
of a CIA unit responsible for snatch-and-grab operations.
Osborne had left the Agency to work as a mercenary,
fighting in various conflicts around the world. They didn't
speak often, but when they did, they raised hell like brothers.

Raven tried calling but only connected with Aaron's
voicemail. He decided to prowl some of the Paris mercenary
haunts to see if he could find him.

And if he couldn't find Aaron or anything else of interest
after a few days, he'd return home to Stockholm. The call to
action would find him anywhere.

As it turned out, Raven didn't make it home for several
more weeks.

IT WAS hard work visiting bars in Paris, enjoying the scenery, the people watching, catching odd glances here and there. The women looked at him, but so did the men, though not the same way. The men had the same appearance as Raven. Military bearing, eyes always scanning, watching for threats though they were far from battle. Paris remained the city where mercenaries congregated between jobs and made themselves available for new contracts. Raven didn't know what was so special about Paris, and no merc he ever asked had an answer, either. They simply *knew*. You want merc work, hang out in Paris. He suspected the tradition began after World War II. Paris was an easy place to be when you had no country to return to. Or didn't want to go home. Judging by the crowds, a lot of mercs were currently between contracts.

Raven sat in a dive called Jean Pierre's, one of those blink-and-you-miss-it spots on a side street not traveled by tourists. The bar catered to the kind of clientele looking for action, and not the female variety. None of the rough-looking men would refuse female company, but they wanted work, too. Raven saw a lot of hard faces, fighters who had seen every horror the world had to offer yet kept going back for more. It wasn't a love of war which kept them returning to the battlefield, but instead a love of action. The love of challenging oneself to survive in situations where the odds were next to zero. Victory didn't come with defeating an enemy; it came from surviving. Survival was victory. If you survived long enough, you died an old man in bed, the ultimate victory, achieved by only a few.

A glance in the mirror behind the bar revealed Raven's countenance matched those around him. He hadn't noticed; if he had, he'd paid little attention. Maybe he should start. The softness of youth was gone. The years were catching up, war without end taking a toll, showing beneath the skin. Too much war. Too much killing. Too many nights hiding in the shadows. He didn't fight because he liked to; surviving only meant the war continued. Raven had no idea what future victory might look like, but he had his reasons for continuing, and they were enough to keep him going despite the wear and tear.

Raven swallowed a mouthful of beer. He'd come looking for an old pal and wound up taking self-inventory. He didn't like what he found and wanted to stop thinking.

It wasn't the life he wanted or chose, but there had been no option after what he truly wanted vanished in a river of blood. Victory might happen when the ghosts stopped talking, but what would he do after?

Raven finished the beer and waved for another. He had to stop thinking and fast. No Zenya to distract him this time. He looked around some more.

Jean Pierre's was narrow in front, where the bar was, and wider in back, where the booths waited. In some of the booths, conversations took place. Men leaned close, talked in hushed tones, and appreciated the lack of light in the rear. Nobody who knew what was good for him stared, so Raven looked away.

A blonde waitress in ripped jeans and a tight Tee-shirt, her thick blonde hair bouncing, carried a tray shoulder high. She delivered drinks to four men playing pool and snapped obscenities at one who tried to grab her rear end. Pivoting, she returned to the bar to fill another order. The two bartenders, both with thin dark hair, served customers along the counter.

No jukebox blared. Raven wasn't sure there was a jukebox. He liked to think if there had been one, somebody put a bullet in it, because jukeboxes were the most annoying machines on the planet. The only noise was the crush of voices and clacking of sounds from the billiard tables.

A heavy hand landed on Raven's left shoulder. Raven, startled, turned his head. A man sat on the stool to his left. Aaron Osborne said, "I never thought I'd see you sitting in a bar without a woman."

Raven laughed. It was as if the time between their last visit had only been a few days earlier instead of a few years. Raven silently chided himself, though. He should have been alert instead of lost in so many thoughts.

"The waitress over there," Raven said, gesturing at the never-stopping blonde, "already told me to go to hell."

"It's okay. She told me the same thing once." Osborne asked the bartender for a beer and a shot of whiskey. Raven drank down his second and asked for a third. He and Osborne shook hands with big smiles.

"You doing all right?" Aaron said.

"Okay. I was already with a woman, by the way. Crazy Ivan named Zenya."

"Can't wait to hear about her. What brings you to Paris?"

"The Crazy Ivan. She's gone now, left this morning. When I realized we hadn't talked in a while I thought I'd try and find you. Ever answer your phone?"

"Not lately," Aaron said.

"What have you been doing?"

"I've spent the last six months guarding oil rigs in the Med."

"You don't like being on water."

"I hate it. Some nights it would have been easy to jump over the edge and drown. Hell with it."

"Why rigs?"

"Only job I could get!" Aaron threw up his hands in frustration. "It's been tough. See all these guys here? Everybody's looking for work and there isn't much to go around. You take what you can get. After six months I quit. I'd rather starve."

"Are you starving?"

"Not yet but money's low. I'll be starving by next month."

Their drinks arrived and Aaron snapped back the shot. He toasted Raven with his pint and they drank.

Raven studied Osborne. He looked tired. He still wore the close-cropped GI haircut, but there was less hair on top of his head. He matched Raven's height but was a little leaner and narrower. Raven had seen how those who underestimated Osborne's stature fared in a challenge. There weren't many who survived to take him on again.

He was always sweating, though. His dome reflected a bright sheen; a trickle or two ran down his temples. In cooler environments, the sweat was minimal. Put him somewhere humid or hot, and he drenched his shirts. Raven once suggested he get checked for hyperhidrosis, but Osborne waved it off. He said he only sweated when under stress. Based on the wetness on his forehead and shirt collar, Raven wondered what stress he might be feeling.

Going broke with no sign of work was enough to make anybody jumpy, though. And Raven wondered if his friend's problem was the call to action he was waiting for.

Raven said, "If you aren't working, what are your plans?"

Aaron drank some beer. "Well, there is something I'd like to talk to you about."

"Okay."

"Let's get breakfast tomorrow and I'll give you the rundown. This isn't the place. I'm really glad you showed up, Sam."

"Anything for a pal."

"In the meantime, let's ditch this joint and I'll show you where some real tough guys go for their drinking."

"You looking to get into a fight?"

Osborne laughed. "If I haven't split a face open by two a.m., I'll be very disappointed."

They finished their drinks. Osborne dropped a large euro note on the bar and set his empty pint glass over the bill. Raven followed him out.

4

OSBORNE WAS SIMPLY ANOTHER MEMBER OF RAVEN'S GROUND Branch team until he saved Raven's life.

Osborne was the new guy, newly recruited by the CIA from Marine Force Recon. To Raven, the first day they met, he was a replacement. A nobody. His team had lost two guys the previous week; the brass picked Osborne to fill the gap. Raven figured if he carried his share of the load, Osborne might do well. Most Marine Recon personnel performed admirably in Ground Branch. Others, not so much. They passed through Ground Branch with motives other than getting the job done, Army, Navy, and Marine hot shots who wanted to turn their "covert action career" into an exploitable property for Hollywood. Working for Ground Branch gave them "street cred" to brag about. The CIA had its share too.

Raven found such characters disagreeable. "Covert" meant keeping your damn mouth shut about what you did, not signing a book deal or becoming a Tinsel Town "consultant" looking for sycophants to tell you what a bad ass you were. Luckily, those types didn't last very long. Sometimes they went home in body bags.

With his "let's break in the new guy" attitude, Raven and his team set out to perform a routine snatch-and-grab. Their target was an insurgent leader and bomb maker named Ameer al-Ghazi. Al-Ghazi not only built improvised bombs, but taught others how to make them, too. His devices had killed and maimed too many US and allied soldiers; the brass decided it was time for him to go. If he could be brought in alive, they'd pick his brain and squeeze every last ounce of information from him and then punch his ticket. If they failed to take him alive, nobody would lose any sleep.

Three a.m. The streets empty, the city quiet, and a crisp 54-degrees with light wind. The kind of night where the Middle East seemed like a nice place to live. Raven and his team traveled in two Oshkosh L-ATVs (Light Combat Tactical All-Terrain Vehicle). Four men to each vehicle. Raven rode up front. Osborne sat in back next to Max Buckley, another member of the team, while driver Ace Higgins sat at the wheel.

Raven sat with his automatic rifle in his lap. Behind him, following a GPS course on a laptop, Max Buckley called out: "Fifty meters ahead." The glow of the screen lit his face.

They'd left the city limits. Most of the surrounding terrain was open desert with a few structures scattered about.

"Pull over here," Raven said to Higgins. He spoke into his com unit, "Team two, hang back. We're going to check the house."

The other team copied.

Raven turned to Osborne and said, "You ready, Marine?"

"Got an itchy trigger finger and I'm tired of waiting," Osborne said. He kept his attention out the window. He looked confident. To his credit, he didn't talk much, or ask too many questions. He'd listened to the briefing and repeated the mission goals when Raven asked. So far, so good. The remainder of the night would tell the rest of the story.

The driver slowed and turned off the road into a cluster of trees. Raven, Buckley, Higgins, and Osborne slipped out of the vehicle. Raven spotted the other L-ATV about 100 yards away.

The four men crossed the dirt road. The target house, lit inside, was a single-level with bullet-scarred walls. In the dark, the house looked as if duct tape held it together. It did not inspire structural confidence.

From a ditch fifteen yards away, Raven scanned the porch through night-vision goggles. He was looking for a slash of infrared paint. Their informant had instructions to apply the paint to the door post if al-Ghazi was at the house.

He spotted the slash to the left of the doorframe.

"Target is inside. Team two, move in and cover us."

Raven, Buckley, Higgins, and Osborne made a final check of their weapons and prepared to the assault. They left the ditch and advanced at a slow pace across the open ground. Their boots crunched lightly on the dirt. Raven and Buckley reached the door first and stood to one side. Higgins and Osborne lined up on the other side. Higgins approached the door and applied an explosive to the doorknob. He rejoined Osborne, counted with three fingers, and pressed a detonator. The blast ripped the door from its hinges and sent it spinning away.

Raven entered first, weapon at his shoulder. He sensed the others moving in behind him.

The front room presented targets right away. Raven opened fire with two-round rapid bursts, tagging the insurgents sitting or standing. They appeared dazed from the shock of the explosion. More shots cracked behind him. The insurgents dropped with no time to react.

Buckley and Higgins broke off for a hallway. Raven and Osborne moved through a doorway into the kitchen.

Raven went left, Osborne right, both scanning for targets. "Clear," Raven said.

"Clear," Osborne echoed.

They left the kitchen for the hallway where the other two were about to check a room. Higgins tested the doorknob.

Automatic fire roared on the other side of the door. The shots punched through the sheetrock and splintered the door and cut down Higgins and Buckley. Both men screamed as the fire continued, then stopped. Raven ran forward with Osborne keeping pace. Raven chucked a grenade through a gap blown in the door. The blast shook the house. Raven pushed open the door.

Bingo. Bomb factory. Tables loaded with half-completed explosive devices. Two had cracked in half from the grenade blast and lay askew, the contents of the tabletops spilled on the floor. Two other tables remained. One body on the floor. The man clutched his now-empty Kalashnikov. Raven headed for one of the split tables. He thought he spotted a leg sticking out from one side. He shoved the broken half out of the way. The man on the ground was already dead.

Neither man was Ameer al-Ghazi.

"Where the hell is our target?" Raven snapped.

"Must have made a beer run," Osborne said.

Raven didn't laugh. He told Osborne to help with Higgins and Buckley. Higgins was silent; eyes closed. Buckley was awake, hands pressed to his body to stop the bleeding. Raven tossed a grenade down the hall to deter anybody hiding. The explosion rocked the walls and pushed a cloud of smoke through the hallway. He grabbed Higgins while Osborne carried Buckley. Raven called team two for help. The four shooters were outside when Raven and Osborne emerged. He ordered them to get Higgins and Buckley to the other L-ATV while they searched the rest of the house for al-Ghazi.

Raven and Osborne reentered with caution. With no second floor, at least they didn't have to worry about somebody coming from upstairs. The narrow hallway presented problems of its own. Raven took one side, Osborne the other. Their muzzles probed the darkness and the lingering smoke.

Raven opened a door on his side and slipped inside. Small bedroom. An empty cot and closet. He rejoined Osborne in the hallway. They checked the next room. No sign of al-Ghazi or any other insurgent. Raven turned his attention to the last room at the end of the hall.

"Get down!"

The muzzle flash from Osborne's weapon filled the dark space as Raven hit the floor. He turned back to look. From the first room he checked a man stumbled out, letting go of a pistol as he hit the floor.

Raven jumped up and ran to the fallen man. Osborne's salvo had opened his chest; there would be no saving this one. He shined a light in the dead man's face. "Jackpot," he said. "There's our target."

"But how? You checked the room!"

"Cover me," Raven said. He entered the room again and found the answer. A trap door in the floor of the closet. He shined the light into the gap but saw no other threats. Dropping a grenade down the hole, he stepped back as the blast sent chunks of debris and more smoke into the room. Waving a hand in front of his face, he turned to Osborne.

"I owe you one," he said.

"I turned to look just in time," the former Marine said. "He was going to shoot you in the back."

"Let's go, Osborne. You'll be one of us yet."

Buckley survived his wounds; Higgins did not. But Raven was happy with Osborne as a replacement. He immediately considered him a permanent member of the team.

Their bond forged over the next three months and many similar missions. Osborne ended up being more than another shooter. His father owned Osborne Defense, and manufactured many of the explosive devices the team used to carry out their missions. They were able to experiment with new gear as a result and report back to HQ what worked and what didn't. When Raven rotated home, they remained in touch. As each traveled their own path in the shadow world, their reunions were few and far between, but they always made the best of it when they did see each other.

Now they were together again. Osborne needed help, and Raven owed him a favor.

5

OSBORNE DIDN'T SPLIT ANY LIPS OR FACES ON THEIR continued sojourn through Paris nightlife. Osborne laughed it off. Maybe next time.

They'd split a taxi to Raven's hotel. Osborne promised to meet Raven in the hotel restaurant at ten a.m. Raven ventured downstairs after a night of restlessness. He couldn't stay out late like he used to. Another sign of getting older. He hated it. His watch showed 9:45 and his goal was to secure a table. He stopped in surprise when he found Osborne already seated in a back corner.

"Hard night, old man?" Osborne laughed.

Osborne sat with his back to the wall. He had a big grin on his face as Raven joined him. Raven's back faced the open restaurant. It made him a little nervous but he had Aaron to warn of incoming threats. Then he chided himself for being paranoid. Nobody was going to shoot up the restaurant.

"You out-drank me last night," Raven said. His head hurt. He grabbed a glass of ice water already on the table and took a long drink.

"And I still beat you here." Osborne held a mug of coffee in both hands with his elbows on the table.

Raven laughed instead of trying to argue. "I'm still worn out from the Crazy Ivan I told you about."

"I'll keep an eye out for her."

The air-conditioned restaurant cooled Osborne considerably, but he still wore light clothes, jeans and a black Tee-shirt. Raven noticed the Rolex Sea Dweller on Osborne's wrist and held out his arm to show his own. "Didn't notice last night."

"Yeah. I bought it when I was doing better than I am now."

A waitress with short dark hair asked for their orders. She wore thick makeup with a silver nose ring in her left nostril. The tips of her dark hair were pink. Raven needed time to review the menu and asked for tea. She departed.

"All right, you promised me a story or something." Raven scanned the list of omelets. "Let's hear it."

"I need your help."

"I'm listening."

The waitress returned with Raven's tea and they ordered. The restaurant wasn't full but they were far enough away from other patrons to not have to speak low. Osborne set his coffee down and leaned forward.

"I need to get back to basics."

"What do you mean?"

"The fighting has to stop sometime, right? And I don't mean war fighting. I need to make peace with my father. He and I have been fighting long enough."

"I don't think you ever told me," Raven said, "how the two of you stopped getting along."

Osborne sat back and shrugged. "It was mostly my fault. He tried to help me after the war. I tried working for the company. I really did. But I couldn't settle down. The war might have been over for me, but I still needed the action. So I quit. I asked my father for some money, a good deal of money, which he agreed to give me, and took off. We haven't spoken since. Both of us said some things I don't think we meant. You know."

Raven nodded.

"And now? The younger guys are working for less. There are more lines on my face every day, and I can't keep this up forever. It's time for a change. Open a bait shop or something." He laughed nervously.

"Think you can settle down this time?"

"It's odd," Osborne said, "what we're opposed to when we're young seems mighty tempting once the joints start to ache a little."

"Sure."

"Anyway, I don't want to go back to Dad empty-handed. I figure I owe him the money he gave me."

"Can we cut to the chase, Aaron?"

Osborne laughed again. "You never were a patient man, were you?"

The waitress returned with breakfast and the two began eating. As Osborne buttered a croissant, he said, "France has a huge drug problem, right?"

"Name a country not suffering from a drug problem." Raven swallowed a forkful of scrambled eggs. He'd decided against the omelet. The chef had made the eggs with butter and the taste was amazing. Scrambled eggs never let you down.

"I've picked out a target, a cocaine dealer in Marseille. A guy and his girlfriend. They're sloppy. They think because they have connections they can deal in the open."

"A target?" Raven said. "You want to rip them off?"

"It's all planned out," Osborne said. "All we have to do is take them out, and leave with their money."

"How many guys you got?"

"Just me and my girlfriend and I hope, now, you."

Raven raised an eyebrow. "This sounds crazy, Aaron."

"We don't need a lot of shooters. One night's work. Split the take. I'm not asking you to work for free."

"How nice of you."

"What do you say?"

"Who's your girlfriend?"

"Oh, you'll like her. Her name is Tracy. She's one of us. Military intelligence, various covert jobs, the whole bit."

"Uh-huh."

"She can handle a weapon and knows the drill."

Raven concentrated on breakfast, mixing his eggs and hash browns. "I don't know, bud."

"What's wrong?"

"Are you kidding? The last thing you want are French drug dealers coming after you. Your target is going to have friends and they will want to know who ripped them off."

"You can't live in fear, Sam."

"I don't want to take a bullet in the back, either."

"But I don't—"

"How about this," Raven said. "I'll give you the money. How much do you owe your father?"

"And be in debt to you now?"

"Pay me back with fishing gear when you open your bait shop."

"No, Sam, the whole point is to get the money myself. Show my old man I've learned my lesson."

"Like how to rip off drug dealers? You'll put a target on your old man's back, too. The Pentagon won't like a major defense contractor having a fight with drug dealers."

Osborne pressed his lips together in a frown. He hadn't taken more than a few bites of his meal and it cooled on the plate. "You in or out?"

Raven started to get a bad feeling, and mixed emotions for saying no. All plans had risks. They could lessen the risks by anticipating problems. What sounded like a hair-brained scheme might work if they sorted the issues. And Raven had a hard time saying no to a friend, especially one who saved his life. He said, "I need to know more about your plan."

"Let's finish breakfast and take a walk. I'll tell you everything. Come on, finish your breakfast. It's on me."

Osborne picked up his fork and returned to his food.

6

THEY WALKED ALONG A BUSY SIDEWALK. HEAVY TRAFFIC FILLED the street. Parisians moved at a brisk pace. Obvious tourists blocked the way as they checked maps and phones.

Raven's bad feeling didn't leave him. Osborne wasn't telling him the truth, and his idea of paying back his father had severe flaws. Money was money. Who cared where it came from?

"You expect your father to make a fuss about you coming back?"

"I sure don't expect a banquet in my honor. Like I told you, we didn't part on good terms. It will help if I return the money."

Raven didn't reply. Why was he so focused on the money?

Sidewalk vendors tried to hock their tourist trinkets. They gave up when Raven and Osborne ignored them despite not being natives. The vendors found plenty of other out-of-towners to hustle.

"Your old man would welcome you home without the money, Aaron. You don't need to risk your life."

"You don't know him."

"But I know how fathers feel about their children."

"I suppose you would, huh?"

"Why don't you call him first?" Raven said. "He's worried about you."

Osborne shook his head. "No, I can't. I gotta have the money when I do it."

"Did you leave your father because of something he did?"

"No, nothing of the sort. I left because I needed to."

"Uh-huh."

"Still think I'm crazy?"

The Place de la Bastille loomed ahead, the tall tower in the center of the street stretching to the sky. Vehicle traffic clogged the roundabout encircling the tower. Diners at sidewalk cafes stuffed the sidewalks.

Raven took it all in as more thoughts raced through his mind. Aaron's story carried genuine emotional weight; the type of detail needed to manipulate another party into accepting the premise. Raven didn't want to think his pal was conning him, but had little doubt he was doing so. His refusal of Raven's offer to clear the debt tripped alarm bells. He couldn't chalk it up to simple pride. Aaron could guard oil rigs in the Med for as long as it took to save the money if he wanted. He had a quick fix in mind instead.

What was his true agenda? Osborne's father ran a defense contracting firm. He manufactured ordnance. Explosives, missiles, high tech equipment. If Aaron screwed up and brought heat onto his family, a threat to national security loomed. The French drug cartel could trade getting even for blackmail. And collect US weaponry from a primary source.

Never mind the embarrassment his father's company might face if the police captured Osborne in the middle of his scheme.

Raven needed to know the truth. And it meant helping Aaron get away clean. He owed Aaron for Iraq anyway; this gave him the opportunity to return the favor. Save Aaron's life the way he'd saved his.

Raven's ghosts had called to him; this was what he'd been waiting for. And he finally answered Aaron's question. "Yes, you're crazy. But I'm not going to abandon a pal. Count me in."

Osborne smiled. It was a bright smile and lit up his eyes. It seemed as if a weight had lifted from his shoulders.

Then an explosion rocked the street and flung the two men across the sidewalk.

RAVEN CRASHED into a wheeled cart of tourist trinkets. The cart fell over, landing on top of its owner on the other side. Aaron Osborne hit the wall of a restaurant.

Raven rolled onto his left side, then flat on his stomach, covering the back of his neck with both hands. The shock wave hit hard, pinning him to the ground, nearby glass shattering, debris flying. He couldn't breathe or hear.

The cart owner's cries for help, lost in a fog of post-blast distortion, broke through Raven's daze. He forced together coherent thoughts and started breathing again. A bomb had gone off in the street near the tower marking the location of the Bastille. Raven waited a moment, and then rolled onto his back and sat up. Thick and heavy smoke billowed around them, hanging like white fog. The smoke stung Raven's eyes. He wiped his eyes and looked around. People were running, screaming. Bodies on the sidewalk.

And gunfire. The rapid blasts of automatic weapons. Not close, but not far. From the center of the roundabout at the tower came more screaming.

"Sam!"

"I'm alive, Aaron!"

Osborne crawled beside Raven and helped him to his feet. There were three cuts, from glass, on Aaron's face. "You armed?"

Raven pulled his .45 autoloader from the shoulder harness under his jacket. "Always."

Two stray rounds smacked the restaurant wall behind them. Osborne drew a SIG Sauer P220 and snapped back the slide. "Let's go hunting."

They ran into the street toward the gunfire.

THE CAR BOMB detonated around 10:30 a.m.

In the moments prior, heavy traffic clogged the roundabout at the Place de la Bastille. Patrons filled available seats at the sidewalk cafes.

Nobody paid attention to the white panel van as it entered the roundabout. Everybody noticed when it exploded.

The bright orange flash, followed by the boom of the blast, broke the vehicle into pieces. Deadly shrapnel flew in all directions. Heavy smoke filled the street.

The shockwave lifted the nearest cars off the ground and slammed them into cars behind and beside them. Secondary explosions from those vehicles rocked the street. A mass of twisted steel, broken glass and shattered bodies replaced the dull street routine.

The intersection echoed with panic and loud screams. Survivors began rising from the devastated café fronts.

From another vehicle further back in the congestion, four armed men emerged. Each toted a Kalashnikov automatic rifle. Tactical vests with spare ammunition magazines covered their chests. They shouted "Allah Akbar!" as they advanced, the AKMs spitting flame. The four gunmen walked along the stopped cars without opposition. They fired at will, fueled by the screams of the wounded and those trying to run away.

The jihadists had full control of the killing ground.

And then two Americans began shooting back.

7

Raven and Osborne weaved through the stopped traffic. They fixed their eyes on the four gunmen heading for the roundabout.

There was nothing Raven could do for the dead, but he could stop more from dying.

As he and Osborne hit the street, they pivoted left. The four gunmen didn't spot the Americans right away. Using cars for cover, shouting at survivors trapped within to stay down, Raven and Osborne engaged the shooters.

One of the gunmen spotted Raven, stopped shouting mid-cry, and shouldered his AK to take aim. Raven fired first. The .45 slug punched through the gunner's left eye, crashing through the back of his skull with a spurt of red. The man dropped. One of the other gunners saw him fall, and Osborne took the second man down with a double-tap through the head.

The remaining two stopped shooting and took cover. The screams and cries of victims all around drowned out the echoes of gunfire.

Raven stayed low, advancing a few feet every couple of

seconds, looking over and around cars, his head like a bouncing ball. There was a risk in doing that, but there was no other way to spot the killers. He only had to drop and move before they saw him.

"On your left!" Osborne shouted, Raven mentally noting his friend's position. His peripheral vision didn't allow a glimpse. He rolled across the hood of a car, the two people inside, a man draping his body over a woman, staring at him wide-eyed through the windshield.

"Stay down!" Raven shouted, moving forward, the urge to end the fight paramount in his mind.

Another burst of AK fire cut through the air, but the rounds didn't come near Raven. Osborne was the target. Raven fired over the roof of a car. The gunman's head split open. One more down. One left. The last shooter swung around the bumper of a vehicle two car-lengths away.

He might as well have been at point blank range. Raven pivoted, feeling the heat of the muzzle flash and the first shot whistling past his ear. He closed his finger on the trigger of the Nighthawk .45 and sent two rounds into the shooter's face. The shooter pitched over and fell flat on his back.

"Clear!" Raven shouted.

"Clear!" Osborne echoed.

Raven looked left. Osborne ran toward him and didn't stop. Raven followed him to the opposite sidewalk where they ducked into an alley.

"You hit?" Raven asked. They put their guns away.

"Only scratches."

Raven looked back at the carnage with a pained expression. The heavy smoke continued to drift with the wind. The van still burned. The flames from other cars contributing to the choking thickness. People were on their feet, trying to get the wounded and walking wounded clear of the mess, police sirens wailing in the distance.

"This is awful," Raven said.

"Nothing else we can do, Sam, come on," Osborne said, tugging on Raven's arm. "It's another day in Paris, come on!"

Raven turned and ran with Osborne along the length of the alley.

Osborne suggested Raven return to his hotel and hide out for a while. "I'll go back to my place where Tracy is waiting, and we'll meet up later tonight."

Raven agreed. The pair split.

Back at his hotel, the lobby was buzzing with news of the terror attack. Guests clustered around televisions in the bar. Distracted clerks struggled to keep their focus as they dealt with a line of arriving guests.

Nobody looked at Raven as he crossed the lobby. Smelling of smoke and looking a little rough, he avoided the elevator and climbed the stairs to his floor. Out of breath, he shut himself in his room, took off his clothes, and spent fifteen minutes in the shower. He washed the smoke and street grime off his body while he thought about what happened.

Jihad activity in Europe was out of control. So called "refugees" from the wars in the Middle East often contained jihadists using true refugees to infiltrate the continent. They made their presence known with random violence and organized attacks. The politicians did nothing, claiming action would discriminate against the refugees seeking a new life. Caught in the middle were the civilians who died as a result. The situation made Raven furious. It was more important to protect killers than victims. Why? Europe had dealt with terrorism for decades, in much better fashion than present-day attitudes allowed.

It was as if governments fed off the conflict, used it to justify endless war and military spending. War was a source of millions of dollars which flowed into the pockets of the corrupt. It served their interests to keep the chaos going.

Raven turned off the shower in disgust, dried off, and pulled on fresh clothes.

He stood up and paced a moment. He'd eaten breakfast not long ago, but felt starved. He called room service and asked for an early lunch.

TRACY DONAHUE, Osborne's girlfriend, jumped when the apartment door opened.

"Honey?" Osborne called.

"Aaron!" She ran to him, crashing into his arms. She felt tiny and fragile because of her petite frame, but she was fit and well-muscled, with long dark hair and big brown eyes. She stepped back and her eyes widened as she saw the cuts on his face. "You're a mess!"

"I was there when the bomb went off."

She gasped and put a hand to her mouth.

"I'm fine," he said, pushing past her into the living room. She had the television tuned to a news report. He switched off the set.

"Did you—"

"Sam and I, yeah. We got four of them." He removed his jacket and pulled off the shoulder harness holding his gun. Setting the rig on the coffee table, he went to the bathroom and splashed his face with cold water to get rid of the sweat. Using a washcloth to dry his face, he avoided his eyes in the mirror. He didn't want to look at himself.

He'd fed Raven a pack of lies and his loyal pal accepted the meal. He told himself it was the only way to accomplish his objective. He shouldn't feel guilty. But he did feel guilty. Raven didn't deserve to be caught in Aaron's scheme. If he'd been able to recruit others to help, he wouldn't have needed Raven.

He finally dropped onto the couch. Tracy squeezed beside him and ran a hand through his hair.

"I'm okay, babe," he said. He eyes stared at a wall, not at her.

"What did your friend say?"

"He'll help us."

"That's good, right?"

"I wish I had more gunners on our side, but nobody wants the job."

"Then it's only us," she said. "We'll get it done and take the money to your father."

Finally, he turned to her, slipping an arm around her shoulders. He pulled her close. "Yeah. It's time to go home. I'm tired of people shooting at me."

He'd told her the same lies. She had no reason to think he wasn't telling the truth.

Tracy laughed. "You act as if this happens every day."

"It's happened enough."

"When do we see your friend again?"

"His name is Sam."

"When do we see him?"

"Tonight."

8

Tracy thought, *Good.*

With Sam Raven along, she could finally learn what her "boyfriend" was up to and why the CIA wanted him stopped. It had been a long three months since her briefing at CIA headquarters. It had been a long three months pretending to be Aaron Osborne's girlfriend. In both instances, she'd yet to learn anything.

She'd met her boss, Christopher Fisher, in his office. Fisher was the CIA's Deputy Director of Operations. She had recently completed an assignment overseas and was looking forward to time off, but Fisher told her she was the only one who could step into this new situation.

Fisher clicked a file folder on his desktop monitor and opened a picture. He rotated the wide-screen display so both he and Tracy could see. The photo showed a side profile of a man with receding dark hair and a sharp jaw.

"Remember him?" Fisher said.

"Aaron Osborne," Tracy said. "His father is Mark Osborne, CEO of Osborne Defense. They build bombs for the military. I met him in Afghanistan. He used to joke that he could get stuff for our unit at cost."

"Uh-huh." Fisher frowned as he studied the picture.

"We dated once, too," she said. "Not long. What's the problem?"

"Mr. Osborne has been overseas the last several years working as a mercenary."

"So?"

"He's lately tripped a couple of alarms and we're concerned he's up to no good."

"What happened?"

"One of our surveillance teams spotted him in a bar last week, talking with a mercenary recruiter. He wants to hire some guys for a job."

"He's recruiting?"

Fisher nodded.

"What for?"

"All we know is he was asking for the names of qualified fighters. For what, we don't know. Since he's an American and his father is plugged in with the military and especially the Pentagon, there could be a national security risk if he's planning something illegal."

"Did our team stay with him?"

"Enough to know where he is right now. You two get along when you dated?"

"Very well," Tracy said.

"Who broke it off?"

"I did."

"Why?"

She shrugged. "Wasn't working for us. We were both gone all the time and barely saw each other."

"Would he give you a second chance?"

"If it's what I need to do to find out what he's doing," she said, "I can make him change his mind."

"Think he might take you into his confidence?"

"I'll make it happen. When it was good, it was very good. The time apart is what ruined things. We can rekindle. Where is he?"

"Paris. You leave tomorrow morning."

Tracy left her chair. "We'll have a grand reunion and drink all the beer in Paris. Want me to bring you back a souvenir?"

"I've always fancied a mini-Eifel Tower for my desk, sure."

Tracy started for the door. "But one thing, sir." Tracy stopped and turned around.

"Yes?"

"What if he doesn't notice I'm around? It *has* been a few years."

"Make sure he does notice you. I don't know why, but I have a bad feeling about this one."

As she sat beside Aaron on the couch and the conversation with Fisher filtered through her mind, Tracy could only echo his concern.

None of the mercenaries Aaron tried to recruit wanted the job. They said the pay was too small for the effort. Tracy believed they didn't want to risk getting killed in retaliation. It surprised her none had decided to tip off the cartel to what Aaron was doing.

Enter Sam Raven. She knew a little about him, but not much. He had been long gone from the CIA by the time she joined. She'd report to her control in London about the arrival, and see what orders followed. They were close to discovering Aaron's agenda. She hoped they could stop him before he did something stupid.

FORTUN DACOURT TOOK his motto from his first name. It meant lucky. His mother had insisted on the name after being unable to conceive for so long. Then Fortun came along and brought them the happiness which had eluded them for so long.

He glanced at the tall woman next to him. He'd been lucky for sure when Geneva Ramsden decided to be his one and only. Her blonde hair was perfectly curled and hung below her shoulders. She wore her hair in a different style every day. Today, curls. Her strapless black dress fit her curvy frame and accentuated every attribute. Dacourt knew there were other women around, some similarly dressed, but Geneva was the only one he looked at.

They stood near one of the six marble support columns holding up the overhang of the Opera de Marseilles—the city's ornate opera theater. It was warm night, and Geneva required no wrap; Dacourt, in his tux, felt a little toasty beneath the clothing.

The pre-show reception carried on in the lobby beyond the entrance. Other patrons waited outside on the steps. They drank champagne and ate fancy hors d'oeuvres and bought drugs. Geneva sipped champagne, but Dacourt needed his hands free for business.

"You predicted we'd run out tonight," she said.

"Night is young."

"We've had what? Four customers?"

Dacourt only smiled. "Wait a little longer, hon."

The show for the evening was The Bluebird Castle, a one-act by Bela Balaza about a newly married couple returning from a honeymoon. Dacourt loved opera. The music and visual spectacle swept him into a trance-like state and away from daily cares.

Geneva liked the opera because it allowed her to dress to kill. Dacourt allowed her the opportunity on a regular basis.

But she was correct. He had predicted a rush. The theater doors would open in twenty minutes. He still had plenty of product in his pockets.

He needn't have worried. While the mingling continued on the steps, young couples and a few single men stepped up to say hello and greet them as friends. Their "friends" passed cash.

Dacourt in return passed small bags of white powder.

And pocketed the cash.

These transactions carried on without notice. Dacourt knew how to be discreet. There was a reason he wasn't behind bars or sitting in front of the interrogation lamps of the narcotics detectives.

Dacourt's customers were mostly young people in their 30s who represented the growing presence of high-tech companies in Marseille. The city's economy, once wholly dependent on the port, was racing into the 21st Century. The influx of young workers, their pockets full of money, with a desire to party, had been a boon to Dacourt's business.

Presently, as Geneva started on her third glass of champagne, the baggies ran out. Dacourt politely turned away business. The people liked cocaine. Dacourt and Geneva liked supplying their cocaine.

"I'll never doubt you again," she said.

"Sure, you will."

An announcement over exterior speakers said the show was about to begin. Wait staff collected empty and half-full glasses. Geneva downed what remained of her third glass in a fast swallow.

In the lobby, the crowd began a slow migration, either straight through the lobby theater doors or up a staircase to the box seats. Dacourt and Geneva climbed the stairs. The couple, their arms hooked, didn't stand out.

"Looking forward to the show?" she said.

"Indeed," he said. "And with all the cash in my pocket, something else, too."

"Barcelona this time?"

"Let's go skiing instead."

"You'll fall and break your arm, dear."

"You better be nearby to catch me then," he said.

Geneva let out a low laugh.

After the opera, while humming a tune from the show, Dacourt steered his Jaguar F-Type into traffic.

"We are out entirely after tonight," Geneva pointed out. She'd taken off her heels. The shoes lay in the footwell of the passenger seat.

"Won't be long till the next shipment. It won't hurt to lay low for a few days."

"How long?"

"Two days. I've already scheduled the meeting at our usual spot."

"We need to change spots. We've used the mall three times already."

"We'll change next time. The mall's convenient for everybody."

"Convenience will get us killed, Fortun."

He patted her leg. "That's why I keep you around. Make sure I don't go soft."

Geneva leaned forward to turn on the radio. A newscast filled the cabin, updates and commentary on the attack in Paris.

"What do you think?" she said during a commercial.

"I'm glad we don't live in Paris," Dacourt said.

He gripped the steering wheel tight for a moment, then loosened his grip. He didn't like an attack on his country any more than the next Frenchmen, and the government couldn't get a handle on the cancer thriving within. Marseille had avoided such incidents, so far, but the city's "luck" could turn on a dime.

Traffic loosened and Dacourt headed for home.

"SAM, THIS IS TRACY."

Aaron Osborne beamed as the petite young woman stepped between him and Raven. Raven shook the dark-haired woman's hand. She wore a tank top and jeans and Raven decided not to challenge her to an arm-wrestling contest. Her handshake was firm and she looked in good enough shape to give him a run for his money. The tank top exposed her tanned skin.

"It's a pleasure," he told her. "Aaron is totally in love with you."

"Hey!"

Tracy laughed. Her big brown eyes widened in delight. "You should hear what he says about me in his sleep."

Osborne blanched and turned for the kitchen. "Who wants beer?"

Both Raven and Tracy signaled the affirmative and Osborne returned with three bottles.

Raven popped off the top of the bottle handed to him, with a sharp twist. Tracy was faster. She downed two big swallows before he took his first sip.

"Nice apartment," Raven said.

"I dare you to make a joke about the closet space," Osborne said.

It was a modest apartment, furnished with the basics, and the pictures on shelves near the wall-mounted television caught his eye. He wandered over. "Who are these people?"

"My family," Tracy said. "I have four sisters."

Raven noticed, but did not point out, Osborne appeared to have no pictures of his family among the set.

Osborne suggested they sit on the balcony. The plastic chair Raven settled on was actually comfortable. Osborne and Tracy pulled their chairs closer and sat across from him. Beyond the iron railing was a pool where kids, watched by lounging parents, played Marco Polo. Even in French, the game was unmistakable. The night was cool.

"We managed to avoid the news," Osborne said. "Nobody's talking about two Americans shooting a bunch of bad guys."

Raven said, "But it won't be long before somebody says something. The cops will want to know who shot the gunmen."

"My contacts in French intelligence," Tracy said, "say it was a local jihadist cell. They've connected the attack with a coded Tweet sent out last week, believe it or not."

Raven nodded. "Decoded before or after?"

Tracy scoffed. "Right? The bodies provided some leads, and they're tracing the leadership of the cell through the Twitter account."

"They'll have cut-outs to hide the origin."

Tracy shook her head. "Don't bet on it."

"Aaron said you were a spook."

She smiled. "INSCOM, Fort Belvoir."

"I did my Ranger training there."

"When?"

"Before you were born, probably."

They laughed.

Tracy said, "And you're ex-Company?"

"Crazy ex-Company," Raven said. "But what I want to talk about is knocking over some drug dealers."

Aaron elbowed Tracy and she transferred her beer from

her right hand to her left, and dug a cell phone from the back pocket of her jeans.

"She'll show you the targets," Aaron said.

Selecting the photo gallery, Tracy handed the device to Raven and told him to scroll through.

Pictures of a man and woman, neither of whom tripped any recognition in Raven's mental mug file, filled the small screen.

"They aren't major players," he pointed out.

Osborne and Tracy said nothing.

The photos showed the couple either together or alone, going about daily activity.

The woman was tall and curvy with blonde hair never in the same style twice. The dark-haired male matched her in height and looked lean; a shot of him without a jacket revealed a muscular upper body.

"Who are they?"

Tracy said, "Fortun Dacourt and Geneva Ramsden. They're tied in with the major syndicate in Marseille. Basically, they're street pushers catering to the new money in town. The tech crowd, stuff like that."

Raven handed back Tracy's phone. "I imagined the target a little bigger. The three of us shouldn't have too much trouble against those two."

"There will be more the night we make the hit," Osborne said. "Dacourt and his girlfriend will meet a syndicate delivery crew at an out of the way place. It's been a mall parking lot the last few times. In exchange for the new shipment, Dacourt hands over the syndicate's cut of recent sales."

"The money we want is in Dacourt's case," Tracy added.

Raven nodded. "How many on the delivery side?"

"Usually four," said Osborne, "three of which carry submachine guns. Dacourt doesn't carry but Ramsden usually has a pistol. Not sure about the fourth syndicate man.

He keeps his hands free for the money and drugs but I'm sure he's armed too."

Raven swallowed more beer. "You sure this is worth it?"

"I'm sure," Aaron said.

"All of them need to be killed, Aaron. If even one survives, you two are on the run, and the syndicate won't get tired."

Osborne shrugged. "We better not miss."

"All I have is my pistol," Raven said. "What kind of hardware are we bringing to the party?"

"It's inside," Tracy said.

9

Osborne pulled a case from beneath the messy bed in the master bedroom. He didn't care about the rumpled sheets. Tracy tried to straighten up as Aaron popped the locks and lifted the lid.

Three automatic rifles sat in foam cutouts, along with magazines and sighting accessories. Osborne grabbed one of the weapons and held it up for Raven to see.

"Galil ACE31, short-barrel, 7.62x39 and takes Kalashnikov mags. Folding stock. It will conceal under a trench coat."

Raven took the offered weapon. Manufactured by Israel, Raven knew the Galil well. The new ACE31 felt lighter, the short barrel a bit of a minus in his book. It measured eight-and-a-half inches and he'd have preferred at least 16-inches for the rifle cartridge the gun fired. But the length would suffice to get the bullets on target at close range. He didn't figure they'd be making 300-yard shots at Dacourt and his girlfriend.

Raven tucked the stock into his shoulder and aimed at the opposite wall. The iron sights looked good, but infrared optic sights sat in the case. He'd attach one to the upper Picatinny rail. He folded the stock against the receiver and extended the Galil in both hands.

"Looks all right," he said.

Tracy stopped fussing with the bed. "All right?" she said. "It's terrific. We tested each gun with 200 rounds."

Raven handed the short-barreled rifle back to Osborne.

"I was going to ask if you had."

Osborne returned the Galil to its foam cutout and shoved the case back under the bed.

"A few more questions," Raven said. "How long have you been watching Dacourt and Ramsden?"

"Three months," Osborne said. "They're resupplied once a month."

"Where?"

"I told you, a mall in Marseille."

"Have you been there?"

"Twice."

"Did you watch the drop take place?"

"We did," Tracy said. She folded her arms.

"Tell me what you saw."

"Dacourt drives a black Jaguar," she said. "Geneva is always in the passenger seat."

"And she has the gun?"

"Yes," Osborne said.

"What kind?"

"Machine pistol," Tracy said. "Beretta 93R."

"Nice piece," Raven said. "All right. What vehicle meets them?"

"White panel van," Osborne said. "I've secured a matching model."

"We're taking the place of the delivery crew?"

"Right. It will keep them off guard and we'll ambush them at the last second."

"I'll drive the van," Tracy said. "You two will set up near the Jag. Dacourt's car sits lower than the van so he has to get out to trade his money for the drugs. Geneva gets out too and stands near the hood of the car."

"And while they're exposed," Raven said, "we take them out and take off with the money."

"Yes."

"What if they change the meet?" Raven said. "Are we prepared to start over with a new plan?"

"Shit happens," Osborne said. "If they don't show up, we know where they live."

"Okay," Raven said. He paused. They'd answered the questions satisfactorily, but he still wanted to find a hole in the plan. Not to lord it over them, but to find a solution. At this point, they'd indeed worked out a sensible ambush.

"What about the other van? Do we know where it starts from?"

"No," Tracy said.

"Then this operation depends on getting there early," Raven said, "and out before the cartel crew shows up."

"Yes," she said.

"And we'll let them find the bodies? Because there's your problem. What if they show up early?"

Osborne laughed. "They're usually late."

"What about the mall? Security cameras?"

Osborne answered. "Dacourt parks the Jag at the far end of the lot. There are security cameras on the exterior of the building, but we'll be too far away for a clear picture."

"What's around the property?"

"Couple of office buildings, which will be empty," Tracy said. "There's a neighborhood, too."

"A neighborhood? In other words, we'll wake up a bunch of people who will call the police."

Osborne said, "They wake up, take a minute or two to

realize what's going on, and then call. It'll be five minutes before anybody calls, and another three minutes before the police get there."

"No," Raven said. "Everybody's on edge after the car bomb. Cut the time in half."

"Dammit, Sam—"

"Hey! You want this to work, or do you want to screw it up? I'm trying to help you."

"Sounds like you're trying to talk us out of it."

Tracy said, "Aaron—"

"I know you think this is crazy, Sam, but don't act like I'm a green rookie."

"If you'd take my offer, we wouldn't have to do this at all."

"We *are* doing this!"

"Then plan on a faster police response!"

"Stop it, both of you!" Tracy shouted.

Raven and Osborne locked eyes, both waiting for the other to respond. Raven held his ground. A trickle of sweat ran down the side of Osborne's face. He wiped it away.

"Fine," he said. "You're right. The cops *might* show up faster."

"The rest of the plan sounds okay," Raven said, "but my offer is good up to the last minute."

"What offer?" Tracy said.

He turned to her. "I told Aaron I'd give him the money."

She looked at Aaron. "And you said no?"

"I have to do it this way, honey."

"Why?"

"I'm done explaining myself," Osborne said. "If you two want to back out, it's up to you."

Tracy glanced at Raven. Her eyes pleaded with him to do something. Raven's mind went blank. If he hadn't been able to talk Aaron out of the scheme already, what else could he say? It was more evidence Aaron had a hidden agenda, and he wasn't going to discover the truth by arguing.

If he insisted on going forward, there was nothing else to do but follow him. The answers would be forthcoming. As long as nothing went wrong during the ambush.

And it *would* go wrong. There *would* be problems. Always.

"When do we leave?" Raven said.

"Tomorrow. I have a chartered flight standing by."

"Chartered? Sounds like you thought of everything."

"Better believe it. I have a lot at stake. We can't mess this up."

Raven believed him.

But not necessarily for his stated reasons.

A chartered flight? Was he spending his last dime on the jet, or had he slipped up with his "it's been rough and I'm poor" routine?

Raven wanted to know more about Tracy too. What was her full background? What did she know that he didn't? Aaron hadn't told her about Raven's offer; what else had he hidden from her? What had she tried to communicate with her look?

All Raven knew for sure was he wanted to get this over with as soon as possible, with as little problems as possible, and discover the truth.

"I guess we have it covered," Raven said. "Is there any beer left?"

"Yeah," Aaron said.

They left the bedroom.

AROUND FOUR IN the morning in Marseille, a container ship from Turkey docked at the Port of Marseille. Dock workers spent the day unloading the ship. Derrick operators removed the legitimate cargo but several crew members also carried off smaller containers. Customs crews conducted inspections quickly, taking for granted the smaller containers held children's toys as the paperwork stated.

The smaller containers were placed onto the beds of two pick-ups, which were then driven to a warehouse adjacent to the port property.

At the warehouse, men opened the containers. They transferred bags of cocaine, hidden within plastic dolls, to tote bags.

By morning couriers collected the totes for transport into the city.

"THIS IS MAKING ME NERVOUS," Geneva Ramsden said.

"The crickets are loud tonight."

"It's not the crickets, dear. We are not using this place for a drop ever again."

Fortun Dacourt looked at Geneva as she sat in the passenger seat with the Beretta 93R machine pistol in her lap. Capable of firing semi-auto or three-round bursts, the 93R was good for laying down suppressive fire.

"I won't argue with a woman who has a gun in her lap," he said.

"It's convenient but we're getting careless."

"We have nothing to fear from the police. Our bribes assure us of that."

Geneva laughed. "Did you forget what just happened in Paris? The jihadists can buy more bombs if they steal our money."

Dacourt checked his watch. At least ten more minutes. The faster the deal ended, the sooner Geneva would quit complaining about the drop location. And find something else to nag him about.

Though she did have a point. They'd used the mall location too many times.

He didn't want to push his luck.

Dacourt's Jaguar F-Type sat in the farthest corner of the huge empty parking lot. The multi-story garage on the other side of the complex might have provided more cover, but Dacourt did not like the limited exits. From where they sat, they had four potential escape points.

The bright parking lamps spread throughout the lot at least helped them see anybody coming. There was something to be said about total awareness, even if it also worked against them. An enemy could see them clearly too. The Jag was fast if they required a speedy getaway, and Geneva was a good shot with the Beretta 93R.

Behind them, the crickets chirped, making an awful racket, within a cluster of trees and brush. If they had to escape on foot, they weren't far from a neighborhood where they could disappear. They'd stashed a backup car in the neighborhood for such an emergency.

Dacourt's arm dangled out the open window, which he'd lowered to let in the cool night air. It also allowed him to hear the engine of an approaching vehicle.

"It's time," Dacourt said.

Geneva grabbed the Beretta from her lap and clicked off the safety.

THE LAMP STANDS with their bright tops annoyed Raven to no end. The glare ruined his night vision.

To keep from being exposed, Raven stayed in the shadows of the trees where they bordered the pavement. The Jag, parked face out, sat about fifty yards away. Keeping low, he moved in spurts, using the trees for cover. He was careful of ground shadows cast by the lights in case they concealed obstacles he might trip over. A twisted ankle would wreck the mission quick, and as Osborne said, they couldn't mess up.

When he guessed he was twenty yards from the Jag, he dropped flat on the uneven ground and braced the Galil ACE 31 in both hands. He settled the red dot of the mounted scope on the windshield.

Speaking into the com unit microphone near his mouth, he said, "In position. Two confirmed in the Jag."

"It will be a shame to shoot up that car," Tracy said.

"Where you two at?" Raven said.

"About to turn into the parking lot," Tracy said.

Osborne replied, "Near the rear of the car."

"Dammit, Aaron, I'm in your line of fire."

"Better move, bud."

Raven cursed and scooted deeper into the shadows before rising and advancing again. If he could line up on the passenger side, he'd avoid Aaron's "friendly fire".

Tracy said over the com link, "We have a bigger problem. I think the delivery crew is right behind me."

"They're early," Osborne said.

"What happened to 'usually late', Aaron?" Raven said.

He ignored Aaron's reply as he moved faster, jumping obstacles, ducking others. No more time for careful steps. Then, as he lined up with the Jag's passenger side, he dropped again and sighted on the female in the passenger seat.

"They've noticed both vans and they look nervous," Raven reported.

Tracy was driving the duplicate van toward the Jag with the other van a few car lengths behind her.

The ambush had gone off the rails before it began.

The early arrival of the delivery crew now left them outnumbered, and outgunned, putting the operation in jeopardy, and Raven wasn't sure how Osborne would react. Would he abort, or open fire in desperation, and take the chance of getting them all killed?

Sweat trickled down Raven's neck.

10

"Two vans?" Geneva said.

"We are leaving." Dacourt pressed the ignition button, the big V8 rumbled to life, and he put the gear selector in drive. He stepped on the gas and the car surged forward.

Automatic gunfire slammed into the back of the Jag. Geneva screamed Dacourt steered left and the coupe roared across the pavement. The bright lamps reminded him of their drawback as the glare exposed them.

The right rear tire exploded, the back of the car sinking, the harsh grind of steel rim on blacktop filling the cabin. Geneva twisted around, fighting the seat belt, the Beretta 93R clutched in her right hand.

The Jag fishtailed, Dacourt letting off the gas to turn into the spin, and Geneva pushed the Beretta out her window. She fired two three-round bursts at the tree line. More gunfire struck the Jag, and Dacourt hit the gas again, trailing a shower of sparks as the car rocketed toward the main building. They could put distance between them and the shooters, and slip away once on the opposite side. Then a careful hike to the back-up car.

Dacourt remained calm despite the sheen of nervous sweat on his face.

The exchanges were supposed to be routine.

What had gone wrong?

Tracy's first instinct was to go after the Jag, but Raven and Aaron were turning it into Swiss cheese. There was still the other van to deal with. The drug crew with their automatic weapons took priority.

Her Galil ACE 31 lay on the floor, held upright by the sling she'd looped around the armrest of the passenger seat. A Glock 19X pistol rode in shoulder leather under her left arm.

She swung the van hard left, tires screeching, and braked hard. Throwing the van into park, she grabbed the ACE and jumped out. The delivery van laid a screaming patch of rubber on the ground as the driver braked to avoid a collision.

Tracy ran around the front of her van, the Galil tight to her shoulder, sighting through the optic lens. She placed the red dot on the driver's face.

The ACE bucked against her shoulder as she fired. Two sizzling 7.62x39 projectiles smacked through the windshield and snapped back the driver's head. The passenger leaned out his open window as the van started forward, but Tracy didn't remain in place. She moved in an arc away from her vehicle, making a semi-circle around the side of the delivery van. The Galil spat lead again and again, scoring a headshot on the passenger. She shifted her barrage to the side of the van. The passenger dangled half out of the window.

The van stopped as it bumped against Tracy's vehicle, Tracy continuing to fill the side and interior with hot slugs.

The Galil clicked empty. She ran back to her van for cover while changing magazines. As she slammed the ammunition in place, the drug van's side door slid open.

She advanced to meet the threat. The light from the parking lamps gave her a quick glimpse inside. One man down and bloody, the final gunner, wounded, exiting, his dark eyes on her as he began to step out. He raised his pistol.

Nope. Tracy put two rounds through his chest before a single foot touched the ground and he tumbled back inside.

"Scratch four drug dealers," she announced into the com link.

She spun at the sound of a loud crash, then ran to her van. The Jag had smashed into the mall building. *Targets exiting.*

Jumping behind the wheel, she sped toward the crash, catching sight of Raven and Aaron running across the lot toward the Jag. The brightness of the parking lamps highlighted their positions, which made both men easy targets. When Geneva Ramsden opened fire with her machine pistol, Tracy tensed but did not slow down. Slowing meant Dacourt and Ramsden would get away, and they had to stop them from escaping. Aaron needed the money. She also needed to answer the CIA's questions. Tracy ducked as a trio of 9mm slugs spiderwebbed the van's windscreen.

She corrected and steered toward Aaron and Raven. Why run when you can ride?

THE JAG CRASHING was the best break Raven could have hoped for.

Dacourt had lost control, the car spinning, coming to an abrupt and violent halt when the driver's side fender met the wall.

"Come on, Sammy!" Osborne shouted, racing from his position after the Jag.

"On your right!" Raven advised, sprinting after Osborne, conscious of Tracy firing on the delivery van, then joining the race. She steered the van toward them.

"Coming to you, Sam!" she said. "Side door unlocked."

Raven zigzagged as Geneva Ramsden opened fire. She had exited the Jag and crouched near the door, gripping her machine pistol in both hands. A burst hit the van's windshield. Then Tracy corrected again to put Raven on the passenger side. He grabbed for the handle to pull the sliding door open. It slammed back. He hopped aboard.

"Down, Aaron!"

Ahead, Aaron dropped. Raven extended the Galil in one hand while gripping a handle inside, and returned Geneva's fire. His salvo forced her to scramble to the front of the car.

Tracy slowed for Aaron. Raven jumped back to allow Osborne space to board.

"Let's go!"

Tracy stomped the gas.

———

GENEVA RAMSDEN EXITED the Jag first, the Beretta in her hand spitting fire. With three incoming targets, she aimed wildly, none of her rounds connecting, though she did impact with the front windshield. Hitting the van didn't count; she wanted the people inside.

When a hail of return fire smacked the body of the Jag, she scrambled for the front bumper. The wall prevented her from moving further back.

"Fortun!"

Dacourt finally made it out on his side of the car,

awkwardly wielding a black briefcase. The money. He jumped onto the hood, and slid in front of Geneva, yelling for her to follow him.

The lights of the incoming van centered on them, and a shot cracked, and Geneva screamed.

11

DACOURT DROPPED THE BRIEFCASE AND GRABBED GENEVA WITH both hands. He hauled her against him, using his right arm to hold her close while snatching the Beretta with his left. He fired the machine pistol until the slide locked back. The oncoming van swerved, then turned in a circle. Dacourt used the opportunity to urge Geneva forward.

She stumbled, dragging Dacourt down, and he dropped the pistol to get her upright again. He made for the corner ahead, Geneva finding some strength to keep up. They rounded the corner and merged with the shadows.

Geneva's legs gave out and she pulled him down once again. He stretched her out on the concrete. She let out a cry. A single shot had gone through her lower back and out her belly. Blood soaked the front of her blouse, her face blank but her eyes wide and full of fear.

On his knees, Dacourt looked over her with a sense of helplessness and panic. He had no weapon and the van screeched to a stop on the other side of the building. A door opened and footsteps scraped on the pavement. Sweat dripped into his eyes as he watched the corner. The killers were sure to come around and finish them off.

Geneva cried out again. He wiped her face with his hand. If they were going to die here, they'd die together.

Footsteps scraped again. A door slammed. The van's engine raced, tires chirping, and the sound of the motor faded. The crickets filled the sudden silence.

Dacourt bolted to his feet and peered around. The bright lamps highlighted the departing van. Its red brake lights flared as it reached an exit and sped off along the road.

Dacourt ran back to his wrecked Jag. The 93R was where he'd left it but the briefcase of cash was gone.

Geneva yelled his name.

He ran back to her. She had an arm beneath her as she tried to sit up. He helped her to her feet and she leaned against him.

"Can you walk?"

"I'll try," she rasped. A line of blood tricked down one side of her mouth.

"We have to hurry."

They started forward, making slow progress, Geneva moving her feet, but dragging most of the time. Dacourt urged her on.

If his luck held, they'd reach the backup car, get help, and then tell the syndicate boss.

And think about getting even.

OSBORNE SHOVED Raven aside and leaped out of the van, ignoring the fleeing couple, and almost tripped in his haste to reach the Jag. Stopping his fall with a hand on the fender, he shuffled around the front of the car, grabbed the briefcase, and ran back into the van. Raven slammed the side door. Tracy reversed and turned the van around toward the exit.

Osborne's rifle clattered to the side as he held up the briefcase in both hands like a trophy.

"We got it! We got it!"

He let out a whoop and laughed.

"Hey, babe?" Tracy said.

"What, honey?" Osborne's grin stretched across his face.

Raven completed her thought. "You better make sure the money's in there." He sat on the floor and placed the Galil next to him.

Osborne's happiness evaporated as he lifted the lid with his hands shaking.

Stacks of euro banknotes of various denominations sat packed inside, wrapped with rubber bands, and Osborne let out a breath.

"Okay, we got it."

Light from the street flashed in the van as Tracy drove.

Raven said, "What didn't we get?"

"What?"

"What *didn't* we get, Aaron?"

"The two pushers, so what? I got the woman."

"Didn't I tell you—"

"Sam, dammit, we'll be out of the country before the bitch is out of the hospital. *If* she survives!"

"You'll never run far enough, Aaron. This whole thing was a disaster."

"What do you know?"

"Enough. And you know better. What's the money for?"

"I told you!"

"What's it *really* for?"

"I *told* you! There is enough here to repay my old man and give you a nice cut, too. More than I thought. Now will you shut up?"

"Uh-huh."

"It's gonna be fine, Sammy, no sweat."

"Really?"

Aaron wiped his face. "*Shut* up."

Osborne closed the briefcase and sat against the wall opposite Raven, clutching the case to his chest like a child holding a teddy bear.

Raven glanced at Tracy. Her concentration was on the road. Back to Osborne. He had his head back and his eyes closed.

Raven had only one thought. *This is the oddest situation I've ever been involved with.*

Tracy parked the van in the empty garage of the home Osborne had rented for the duration of their mission. As the automatic garage door closed off the night, Raven finally allowed himself to relax.

But a nagging feeling told him he wouldn't be at rest for long.

12

THE TRIO ENTERED THE FURNISHED RENTAL WITH THEIR weapons and combat gear. They placed the equipment in a corner for cleaning and sorting later. Tracy announced she was heading for the shower.

Osborne grabbed two bottles of beer from the refrigerator and gave one to Raven. The two dropped onto the couch.

"I'll sleep good tonight!" Osborne said. He took a long drink.

Raven stared at his bottle. He wasn't going to get anywhere with Aaron as far as the money went. Foremost on his mind instead was putting the money somewhere safe. They had to move while evading cartel and police detection. The one good thing about the failure at the mall was Aaron had been correct about the cops. But they'd been close enough to the building for the security cameras to capture their faces.

The cops wouldn't be clueless for long. Ditto the cartel, who probably had enough cops on the payroll to receive advance notice when the police accessed the footage.

Osborne emptied the beer down his throat and let out a loud belch. He turned to Raven. "Want another?"

Raven held up the full bottle.

"Well, hell, Sam, better catch up!" Aaron left the couch for the kitchen.

TRACY TURNED on the shower and set the temperature. As steam covered the bathroom mirror, she leaned against the sink and pulled her cell from a pocket.

She felt sweaty and gross all over, but she had to inform her handler of the latest.

She texted a short message to a number in London.

Got the money. Awaiting next move.

She ended the text with a number. **078.**

The reply: **Raven?**

Still here. He offered Aaron money but Aaron insisted on raid. No clear answer why. Very frustrating.

OK. Stay with it.

Tracy deleted the messages and set the phone on the counter. Then she pulled off her sweaty clothes and stepped into the immediate comfort of the hot spray.

THE DOCTORS DIDN'T ASK questions when Dacourt brought Geneva to the hospital because she was bleeding. He had until surgery ended, one way or another, before they demanded answers he might not be able to give.

Which meant he needed some luck yet again.

He paced the hospital lobby, unable to sit still, pained worry across his face. He'd made a phone call to his police contact as soon as doctors wheeled Geneva into surgery. He was waiting for a call back. He needed Sergeant Bereau to intervene before the questions started.

He jumped and made a startled sound as his phone rang. He dashed to a corner to avoid the eyes and ears of the others in the waiting room.

"Felix?" Dacourt said. "You have news?"

"I have pictures," said Sergeant Felix Bereau, 20-year veteran of the Marseille police force.

"My face?"

"Isn't on them. The angle at which your car crashed kept you off the video. We see a little of Geneva, and a lot of one of the men who attacked you."

"Enough for an ID?"

"His face will be plastered all over by morning."

"You need to forward the picture to *me*, Felix."

Dacourt's voice remained low, but he hissed the emphasis to make it sound as much like a command as possible. With his face in the corner, he still felt eyes on his back. Now wasn't the time for loud threats.

"You'll have it. But it won't help if we can't identify him."

"You have his picture."

"Yes. But there is no promise of his face being in our database, or Interpol's, or anybody else's. We aren't perfect, Fortun. If you want perfection, get shot in America. American CSI can tell you what he had for breakfast and give you his Facebook account."

The sergeant let out a little laugh.

"None of your *jokes*, Felix. Geneva may not make it."

"Uh-huh."

Anger bubbled inside Dacourt, but he took a deep breath, and closed his eyes. After a moment, he opened his eyes and said, "When may I expect you here at the hospital?"

"I'm turning the corner now."

"Do you—"

"I have the picture on my phone. What do you pay me for?"

Dacourt breathed heavily into the phone as he loosened his tight grip on the cell.

Bereau let out another laugh.

Dacourt composed himself, standing erect, shoulders back, tilting his head to look up at the corner where the wall met the ceiling.

"I'll see you shortly, Felix."

Dacourt finally sat and put his face in his hands. His whole body felt dirty, dried sweat grating against his skin.

His legs were shaking, but not from anger at Bereau. Geneva might be dying down the hall. He clung to the idea of no news meaning good news and then he heard Bereau's voice.

He put his hands down and turned his head to the left. At the nurse's station, Bereau had his badge out and spoke with the nurse behind the counter. The young woman pointed at Dacourt. Fortun stood. Felix put away his badge and approached the waiting area.

"I'm here," the sergeant said.

Felix Bereau wore a tan trench coat over a gray suit, dark hair touched with gray. He was two inches taller than Dacourt.

The drug seller had to look up to meet the sergeant's weary eyes.

"Show me the picture."

Bereau pulled a smartphone from inside his coat, opened the picture and showed the screen to Dacourt. "Look familiar?"

"Of course not."

"Just checking." Bereau tapped the screen and entered Dacourt's number and pressed send. When Dacourt's phone chimed a moment later, Fortun examined the picture again.

The image showed the man exiting the van and running to the Jaguar. Light reflected off the sheen of sweat on his forehead. *The footsteps. This was the man who took the money.*

Money Dacourt still owed his syndicate bosses.

"Whoever he and his friends are," the sergeant said, "they won't be able to leave the city or country. This picture will go everywhere."

"Including *my* people," Dacourt said. He stared at the photo.

"Do what you must."

"Excuse me."

Dacourt sat again and forwarded the photo to his primary contact in the syndicate, who would inform the top bosses, who probably already knew about the shooting but hadn't tried to reach him yet.

"I'm getting some coffee," Bereau said.

Dacourt waved him off as if brushing away a buzzing fly.

When the phone rang a moment later, Dacourt moved to the corner again and put his head down.

"Yes."

"The money?" his syndicate contact said.

"Stolen. I'll pull the funds from my account to make up the loss."

"Fair enough, but we can't let this incident go unpunished."

"This is my vendetta," Dacourt said. "Send me a gun crew and I will find this man."

"We will take your request under consideration."

"But—"

"The old man will allow an electronic transfer in this case. You will move our money by five p.m. tomorrow."

"All right. I want—"

His contact dropped off.

Dacourt cursed and put the phone away. He turned

sharply and checked his step. Sergeant Bereau stood behind him, blowing into a steaming paper cup.

"Watch it, Fortun."

"Get out of my way."

The sergeant cracked a smile. Dacourt's attention snapped to the surgeon coming toward them.

13

"Is she—"

"Resting comfortably," the surgeon said. "You can go in shortly. But first—"

Bereau held out his badge. "I'm already here. Let's talk for a minute."

The surgeon led the sergeant back to the nurse's station, where they spoke in hushed tones.

Dacourt dropped into a chair. He was too relieved to care what the surgeon and Bereau had to say.

Dacourt slept in a chair in Geneva's hospital room. She remained sedated and hooked to monitors. The surgeon and attending physician expected a full recovery. She'd be able to leave in a few days, but full recovery would take weeks. Maybe longer.

Back home to shower and eat, Dacourt used his computer to transfer funds to a syndicate shell account. He'd advocated using electronic money transfers many times, but the old school attitude of the syndicate boss, a man pushing 90, had been difficult to surmount. The old man didn't trust computers. But now, since it was an emergency, he had allowed the electronic transfer. Maybe this was the leverage Dacourt needed to make the practice permanent. Had they done this as a matter of habit much earlier, Geneva wouldn't have been shot, and the money not taken.

He called his syndicate contact.

"You're paid."

"Very good."

"You know where my loyalty lies," Dacourt said. "Do I get my shooters?"

"The problem will be taken care of," the contact said. "You will be re-supplied and we expect you on the street."

"Unacceptable!"

In the confines of his home, Dacourt didn't conceal the outburst.

"One moment, Fortun."

Dacourt paced in the narrow kitchen which he'd always considered small, but now felt microscopic. His eyes lingered on a corner near the stove where grime had accumulated. Neither he nor Geneva were the best housekeepers.

"Fortun."

"I'm still waiting."

"In light of your prompt payment of funds, which the syndicate appreciates, you will have the task of tracking your attackers. Whatever money you recover is yours."

"Give the old man my thanks."

"There is also the matter of the drugs in the delivery van."

"Confiscated?"

"Can you recover the product?"

"Sergeant Bereau will see to that."

"You have an opportunity to move up in the organization if you succeed," the contact said. "Don't ruin it."

"Whoever attacked us," Dacourt said, "will pay. I will cut off their ears and wear them as a necklace."

The contact laughed. "Try wearing such a thing to your operas."

"When will—"

"Shortly, Fortun. The shooters will join you shortly. In the meantime, I'd start creating a plan of action."

"Way ahead of you."

Dacourt ended the call and departed for a return to the hospital. He didn't want to repeat Bereau's doubt about the attacker's sweaty face not being in any databases; the face *had* to be. Dacourt needed a place to start. A name to brand into his memory along with the face already there.

RAVEN STEEPED a tea bag in a mug of hot water. He looked up when Tracy entered the kitchen.

"Aaron still asleep?" he said.

"Out cold. How many beers did you two have?"

Raven gestured to the kitchen trash can. Empty beer bottles overflowed.

"I had exactly one," Raven told her.

She shook her head and crossed to the coffee maker. Raven dropped his tea bag on top of the heap of bottles.

Tracy poured her coffee.

"You take it black?" Raven said.

"Black and strong."

Raven let silence pass between them. She'd fought well at the mall. He wondered if she'd seen more combat than the average military intelligence officer, or if there was more to her story than she had revealed.

"I guess you were right," she said.

Raven didn't reply.

"I appreciate you not saying I told you so," she said.

"I'm not sure what to say. Why wouldn't Aaron take the money I offered instead?"

"I don't know," she said. "He hasn't told me anything more than he's told you."

"This makes no sense."

Tracy said, "What do you think we should do next?"

"Get breakfast, I'm starving."

"You know what I mean. We have a briefcase full of cash to hide and the heat's on."

"For sure we can't stay here."

"Uh-huh."

"Let's take a drive to Switzerland."

"Are you nuts?"

"No, my bank is there. Plus, the cops and the bad guys will be looking for us. They're already watching planes and trains and everything else. A road trip will be our best bet for staying off the radar."

"What's the name of your bank?"

"Bergstrom Brothers."

"Never heard of them," she said.

"They're private. *Very* discreet. They cater to people like us."

"What about crossing the border?"

"What about it?"

"We got awfully close to the building, Sam."

Raven shrugged. "I saw the camera and it probably captured a nice view of the van's license plate. We have to ditch the van and alter our appearances. We're only moving a briefcase, not half of Fort Knox."

Tracy nodded and sipped her coffee.

"Where are you from?" she said.

Raven leaned against the counter near the sink. The kitchen's bland white tile and countertops were balanced only by the tan wood of the cupboards. He let his eyes wander around the antiseptic look while he thought about how to answer the question.

"Nowhere," he said. "Dad was an army officer, so we moved around a lot."

A little of the truth wouldn't hurt.

"And you joined because of him?"

Raven let out a breath. How to answer? He didn't want to give her his life story, or even a truncated version. Aaron had most likely told her about their experience together, but Osborne didn't know many details of Raven's past.

He also didn't want to revisit the memories, or the pain associated with them.

"Pretty much," he said instead. "Did a few years in special forces and then CIA."

"Did you get fired?"

"I quit."

"And went freelance?"

"Long story."

"Okay, don't tell me." She laughed, then turned serious. "Can I trust you, Raven?"

"What do you mean?"

"Hey!"

Raven and Tracy turned to the sudden arrival of Aaron Osborne, still wearing his boxers. He looked haggard and still tired despite sleeping through the night.

"Damn," he said. "I got a bitchin' hangover. Bongo drums in my head, man." He laughed.

Tracy handed him her coffee, told Aaron to choke it down, and said she'd get the shower going because he *seriously* needed one. She left the kitchen. Osborne made no move to grab her. He swallowed a mouthful of coffee.

"What are you two scheming about?"

"How to get out of France," Raven said. "After you clean up, we'll get breakfast and figure out what to do."

Tracy returned. "Water's hot." She poured another mug of coffee. Aaron finished the coffee and put the mug on the counter. He snaked his arms around her and playfully suggested she help wash his back, but she gave him a shove. He laughed again and staggered away.

Raven drank his tea and watched Tracy not look at Aaron as he departed. She kept her eyes on the kitchen floor.

"What were you going to ask me, Tracy?"

She shook her head. "Later."

He said okay.

14

AARON DIDN'T WANT TO GO OUT AND EAT. HE STRETCHED OUT on the couch and moaned a lot. Raven and Tracy left to get take-away and brought the food back to the safe house.

Tracy turned on the television. She and Aaron sat on the couch while Raven ate off his lap on the floor. His Styrofoam container of scrambled eggs, bacon, and hash browns formed a greasy mix.

Osborne spoke between mouthfuls of egg. "We gotta ditch the van."

"Read my mind," Raven said.

"What do you think we should do?"

Raven repeated what he'd told Tracy, who focused on eating and appeared to tune out the reprise.

"I don't have an account in Switzerland," Osborne said.

"My banker will get you set up. Won't take more than a half-hour."

Finally, Tracy jumped in. "We have to get there first."

"I'll stay here and plot the route," Raven said, "while you two go get another vehicle. Who rented the van?"

"I did," Osborne said. He shoved a piece of bacon into his

mouth and made big motions with his jaw as he chewed. He dabbed his forehead with a napkin.

"Then, Tracy, you get the other car. And rent from another place, don't double dip."

"Not my first time at the rodeo," she said.

Raven was going to reply when the news anchor on the television began describing the shooting at the mall. Tracy turned up the sound. What the news anchor described, and what interviews with police revealed, suddenly meant little as a picture flashed on the screen. A black-and-white picture of Osborne. The picture showed him running to the wrecked Jag with his Galil in plain view, as well as his face.

"Well, shit," Osborne said.

"Ditch the van," Raven said. "Tracy gets the new vehicle and you keep out of sight, Aaron. Unless you're a master of disguise."

Osborne glared at Raven. "You're acting like you're in charge."

"Apparently I should be."

Tracy wiped her mouth. "No fighting, you two."

Raven said, "Here's a better idea. Tracy and me deal with the vehicles and, Aaron, you plot our way to Zurich."

Aaron put his container of food on the table. He looked defeated. He used the remote to mute the TV. "Okay," he said.

"It's going to be fine," Raven said, "but I told you this might happen."

"You did."

"We should have worn masks," Tracy said.

"It went to hell the moment the delivery crew showed up early," Raven said. "But yeah."

Raven resumed eating. Tracy took her trash to the kitchen. She returned with more coffee.

"How can you keep eating?" Osborne asked Raven.

Raven swallowed a mouthful of hash browns. "Not my first rodeo," he said.

Tracy stifled a laugh.

Osborne's shoulders sank.

GENEVA REMAINED IN BED, stirring only long enough for Fortun to see her notice him in the corner chair.

He jumped up and grabbed her right hand. Her weak grip almost brought tears to his eyes. He clasped both of his hands over hers and she whispered something. He told her to rest and not talk. He told her the doctor said she'd be okay. With a half smile, Geneva dozed off again.

Fortun held her hand a moment longer. At least it was warm. His luck had passed to her.

He released her hand and sat down again, and his phone rang.

"Yes?"

A man's voice. "We are downstairs."

"Who is this?"

The man on the other end said, "You ordered shooters, didn't you? We are in the parking lot. Black Town Car."

Dacourt blasted out of the chair, saying, "Don't move," as he cleared the hospital room doorway. He let the door swing shut on its hydraulic hinge.

Three floors down. Dacourt took the stairs and hurried.

Dacourt found the black Town Car easily. The big four-door dwarfed most of the other cars in the lot. He slipped into the back seat.

Two men up front. They might have been twins. Thin, pale, mustaches, black suits. The driver wore wrap-around chrome-framed sunglasses while the passenger smoked a foul-smelling cigarette. His arm dangled out the open window, but smoke from the lit tip trickled inside.

"No names," the driver said, watching Dacourt in the rearview mirror.

"Okay."

"We will call you; you will not call us."

"Right."

"Where do you want us to start looking?" Sunglasses said. His face looked dull with the shades over his eyes, and Dacourt figured it was an improvement.

"You have the picture?" Dacourt said.

Smoker exhaled a stream out the window. "We got it," he said.

"I had my police contact trace the license plate. It's a rental. A Hertz office." Dacourt took out his phone. "I'll text you the address."

It only took a moment. Sunglasses looked at his phone after it beeped. He showed the address to Smoker.

"Doesn't Yvette work there?"

"Tuesdays and Fridays."

"It's Tuesday."

"Then she will be there."

Sunglasses finally turned his head to look at Dacourt.

"We'll start right now. Get out."

Dacourt didn't say goodbye as he pushed open the door.

Dacourt returned to Geneva's room and used the internet on his phone. He wished the cops hadn't shown his attacker's face on TV. If the authorities grabbed the man first, Dacourt was sure Sergeant Bereau would send him a tip.

He knew they were looking for at least three people. Sergeant Bereau had, earlier in the morning, passed along more info saying the cameras also captured long shots of another man and a female.

They would likely ditch the van, and need a new vehicle with which to escape the city.

On his phone, he studied the routes out of Marseille. Which road would they take? And where would they go?

They might be going anywhere, and in fact might already be gone. He wondered if Sunglasses and Smoker were embarking on a wild goose chase. Should he consider himself lucky Geneva had survived and call it a day?

But what if there was still a chance to catch them?

He'd been lucky so far; maybe his good fortune would hold.

SUNGLASSES AND SMOKER visited the Hertz office located in a shopping center.

They crossed the parking lot resembling the skinny version of the Blues Brothers except they were French drug cartel assassins on a mission from the kingpin.

The inside of the rental office felt chilly with the A/C blowing hard from floor vents. Music from overhead speakers punctuated the conversation between a customer and the office manager at the counter. The manager's name was Yvette.

Sunglasses and Smoker stayed near the door, while Yvette finished the transaction. She was short and stocky, generously proportioned, with her hair pulled tightly back. It was her "office look", coupled with a very conservative blouse-and-skirt combo. Sunglasses knew her as a party girl who only let her mane down, and didn't know the meaning of the word modest, when there was partying to be done.

She acknowledged both with a smile and promised to return quickly as she escorted the customer outside.

Yvette returned on clicking heels after a few minutes. "What do you need?"

Sunglasses did the talking. "Remember this van?" He showed her Dacourt's picture on his cell.

"Yes, it's out for the week."

"Police been here?"

"Not yet."

"Are you the one who signed out the van?"

"No. It's listed on the long-term sheet."

"Do you know if the man in this picture rented it?"

Yvette tapped the computer keyboard on her side of the counter and read off the monitor. The screen reflected in her black-framed glasses.

"American. Aaron Osborne. I'll print his ID for you."

While the printer beside the computer ejected a sheet of paper, Yvette frowned.

"What's wrong?" Sunglasses said.

"I got a call from a friend at our other office this morning, and she asked about the van too. She wanted us to know it might be leaving the country."

"Why?"

"A woman came in and rented a four-door, another American, and when my friend showed the car, she saw the van with our sticker on the back. The van followed the American woman out."

Sunglasses grunted. "How do you know they might be leaving the country?"

"The woman had to buy extra insurance because she was driving to Zurich."

Sunglasses smiled.

15

DACOURT REMAINED IN THE HOSPITAL ROOM CHAIR, WATCHING television while Geneva slept. His phone rang.

"We have them," Sunglasses reported.

Dacourt sat up with excitement. "In front of you?"

Sunglasses explained the new information, adding, "Do you know what's in Zurich?"

"A lot of banks."

"I'm getting more men to help watch those banks. We have IDs on the man in the police photo and we're getting the woman's ID. They won't slip by."

"Unless," Dacourt said, "they know we are looking and they're laying a false trail."

"There is only one way to find out," Sunglasses said. "But we also have names and faces. They won't be able to run for very long, no matter how far they go."

"Do you have the license plate of the new car the American woman rented?" Dacourt said.

"We'll have it soon."

"Send me the information. My police contact can track

them using the speed cameras on the motorways. False trail or not, we'll find them."

Dacourt decided his luck was holding up very well indeed.

MARSEILLE TO ZURICH. Seven hours. They planned to drive in shifts and make the trip with no stops other than bathroom breaks.

Raven drove the first shift, Osborne in the passenger seat, Tracy in back, and nobody spoke. The Volkswagen Jetta wasn't his first choice for basic transportation. He would have preferred something larger with more legroom. On the plus side, but it was fully loaded, GPS, leather seats, decent stereo. At least he figured the stereo was decent. They rode without any music. It was more important to stay focused on the drive while watching for any tails, police or otherwise.

They planned to follow the A7 all the way. Raven didn't like the idea of sticking to one route, but it had the benefit of being the fastest. The sooner they reached Zurich, the better.

Raven felt ready for any "just in case" scenario. His light jacket covered the Nighthawk .45 riding in the shoulder harness under his left arm. The Galil automatic rifles, cleaned and reloaded, sat in the trunk. The briefcase full of money and their minimal luggage rode back there too.

Seven hours.

The outside scenery flashed by.

TRACY, in the back seat, watched Raven drive. She knew more about him than he realized. Maybe later there would be a chance to reveal to him her true affiliation. Her attempt in the kitchen earlier hadn't been a good move. But if both of them had the same questions, what help could he be?

Aaron's plan couldn't move forward without the stolen money. But she still had no idea what plan he had in mind.

She had to find a way to tell Raven why she'd been ordered to get involved with Aaron again and learn his agenda. How could she do so with Osborne so close?

She'd managed to send another text message to her handler in London. She advised of the trip and mentioned she'd committed the unpardonable sin of (a) using her real name to rent the Jetta and (b) telling the rental office of their Zurich destination. She'd been lucky Raven insisted she rent the car alone while he waited in the van. He knew nothing about her choices.

She had her reasons. If she failed to learn Aaron's true plan, fixing things to arrange for his murder would put a stop to whatever he had in mind. She didn't have any moral objections to the plan. She was a covert operative. The mission came first. In this case, protecting US interests from a potentially rogue actor.

Osborne had to be stopped one way or another, and in such a way as to not come back on the United States government. If the trail she'd left allowed the cops or drug thugs to take him out of play, so much the better. It put her and Raven at risk, too, and while she knew she might be able to slip away in any confusion, she figured Raven was smart enough to do the same. Unless his devotion to Aaron prevented him from doing so. She knew their history; the bond between two fighters who had been through hell together was a tough one to break.

Would he side with her if presented with what the CIA suspected?

Tracy let out a breath and turned her head to watch the other cars on the A7.

She'd get her chance to bring Raven up to date if she remained patient.

Unless she ran out of time when the cartel caught up.

AARON OSBORNE SAT QUIETLY in the passenger seat, the A/C vent turned to blow on his neck. He wondered how to get rid of Tracy and Raven.

Tracy had been a fortunate catch. He hadn't wanted their relationship to end when she'd originally broke off with him, and disagreed with her reasons for doing so. But that was life. Meeting up with her again, when neither had demands on their time, had been nice. But now there were demands, ones she didn't know about, and it was time to part again. For good.

They were no longer useful. They were now a threat. The cops and druggies hunting for them made no difference. He'd be going full black soon. Nobody would find him until he was ready to emerge, and by then, he'd have an army to bring his dream to reality.

But he hesitated to plot their murder. Raven was an old friend and Tracy—well, good women were hard to find. But the mission came first.

Just as his father had taught him.

He couldn't afford to let Raven and Tracy live. Once they discovered his plans, they'd try and stop him. Raven for sure. Nothing could stand in his way. Not even a friend or a lover.

ONE HAD to stay with the car at all times at every stop.

At the first motorway rest stop, Raven stayed with the Volkswagen to fill up the tank while Osborne and Tracy used the bathroom. The restrooms adjoined a large convenience store.

Osborne waited for Tracy to enter the ladies' room, then rerouted away from the facilities. He found cover near a cluster of trees behind the store.

He dialed a number from memory. It wasn't a number he wanted on speed dial.

"Yes?"

"Draco. It's me."

"Where are you?"

"On our way to Zurich to deposit the money in a Swiss account. From there I can transfer the funds to you."

"You were supposed to bring me the cash. I don't like this delay," Draco said.

"We didn't get away clean. I still need my shooters."

Draco laughed. "I'm well aware. The cartel is reaching out for freelancers."

"Are you serious?"

"They want Zurich covered. They know you're going there."

A mix of fear and anger flashed through Osborne. "What? How?"

"Don't ask me. I'm not the one who should have planned better."

"Hey! Remember who you're talking to, Draco. Without me you're just another out of work merc with a price on his head."

"No, you remember who *you* are talking to. We can switch you off anytime we like. If you fail to get the money to us, we can cancel the contract the hard way."

"Okay, wait, hang on," Osborne said. "We aren't going to get anywhere talking like this."

"I'm glad your better sense has prevailed."

"The money is on the way, we won't have any trouble

making up the lost time, and we will finish the project on time. Chumachenko has his end covered too."

"If you say so. I don't trust that Russian swine."

"I'll be in touch if I need to update you again."

"Watch out for stray killers, Mr. Osborne."

Osborne bit off a curse and ended the call. He peeked around the tree. Tracy was either still in the bathroom or hadn't yet emerged. He crossed the open grass to the restrooms and slipped inside the men's room. He needed a piss and a splash of cold water on his face.

Getting his picture snapped was a screw up, yeah. But how in the world did the cartel figure out they were going to Zurich?

And could he change their plans without revealing to Raven and Tracy there was more going on than simply depositing the money?

I still need my shooters.

Nuts, he thought. *You're too weak to kill them.*

16

"AARON?" RAVEN SAID. "YOU ALL RIGHT?"

Raven saw Osborne leaning over a sink, his head down. He looked up at Raven in the mirror. He said yes and made a show of washing his hands before brushing past Raven to go back outside.

Raven frowned as his friend exited. Aaron's face had a red flush and he looked angry.

Tracey had returned from her break and volunteered to drive. Raven took his rotation in the restroom and found them both in the car waiting when he returned. Aaron and Tracy weren't talking, and Osborne stared intently out his passenger side window.

Raven climbed into the back seat. Tracy had purchased an assortment of soft drinks and snacks. Raven opened a can of Pepsi and sank into the seat as the Volkswagen powered back onto the roadway.

He watched Aaron, who now had his eyes fixed out the front windscreen, his jaw clenched tight. What had set him off?

Raven drank some more Pepsi and looked out the

window. His danger scan would remain constant from here on out. Unless he'd had a hard time on the crapper, Raven couldn't think of why his friend appeared upset.

As Raven turned his head again, he caught Tracy looking at him in the rearview mirror. He didn't acknowledge, but no doubt she wanted eye-contact. She must have noticed Aaron's mood as well. Great. They both knew something wasn't right. How much longer till he discovered what was happening?

And what did Tracy know about it?

———

AT LEAST THEY had booked a motel for their arrival in advance, Raven thought. Motel One Zurich was affordable for a crew of misfits who allegedly had no money, and Raven quickly found himself in a small but comfortable room with no minibar. He'd have to go downstairs for his evening beverage. He was happy to be off the road.

The window overlooked a quiet neighborhood. The evening twilight made it tough to see the partial view of Lake Zurich the front desk told him he had. He shut the drapes and sat on the edge of the bed.

He didn't like waiting or not knowing the score. A sense of impending betrayal gnawed at him. And he was all alone. No help or backup, and anybody he could call wouldn't reach him in time. He had to wait and let the situation play out.

Could he count on Tracy if Aaron pulled a double-cross?

Why had she asked if she could trust him?

Now he really needed a drink. He found his key card and wallet and went downstairs to the bar.

———

Raven knew how to get to the bank so he took driving duties after breakfast the next morning.

During breakfast, Aaron seemed himself. A bit louder than usual, talking too much, using extra napkins to wipe his sweaty forehead. He was also excited to get to the bank and put the money somewhere safe and be over with the adventure. He said the three of them had tickets for New York. Their flight departed the following morning. He wanted them both to meet his old man and share in the reunion they helped bring to fruition.

It was a long ride through morning traffic to get to Bergstrom Brothers, Bankers. They finally arrived at the single-level stone building off Uetlibergstrasse. There was no parking lot, but a limited number of spaces diagonally in front of the building had two open spots. Raven parked at the end of the row.

The bank was located well away from the major city center, occupying a portion of a block. A semi-circle of trees wound behind the building.

They entered the marble-tiled lobby with its stone pillars. Teller cages and loan officers' desks sat on either side. Raven, having already made the appointment, brought Tracy and Aaron to a corner receptionist. She confirmed the appointment and asked them to sit and wait. They found a soft couch to accommodate the delay. Osborne held the briefcase full of cash on his lap.

Banking matters were private between banker and account holder. Herr Bergstrom stepped through the double doors behind the receptionist. He was a middle-aged man with his dark hair slicked back and perfectly parted. His Savile Row suit was a conservative gray. He shared a moment of greeting with Raven before escorting Osborne, alone, into his office. He closed the double doors behind them.

Raven and Tracy remained on the couch, but Raven didn't sit for long. He told her to follow him and they went over to the entrance, looking out through the glass at the street.

"See something?" Tracy said.

All appeared normal, but something wasn't right. He had the sense they were under a microscope or, worse, in a sniper's line of sight.

Another office building sat across the street, with no identifying markings. An anonymous gray building. But parked beside the building, in the shadow of a side alley, was a vehicle Raven didn't like.

"The black van in the alley," he said. "Tinted windscreens."

"I see it," she said. "We left the weapons in the car."

"I have my pistol." Raven cursed. "How did they track us?"

"Might be nothing," Tracy said quickly.

"And maybe it's the cartel." Raven turned and examined the lobby. He lived by two rules. One: no roots. Nothing to tie him down in one place. Two: no gunfights in public. The danger to innocents was too high. He didn't want a battle in the bank. The line of customers to the teller cages was sixteen-deep. The office workers and loan officers went about their business with whispered chatter. It was another routine day at the bank like so many others. The last thing he needed was to get these people involved in a lethal situation where they had no defense.

Well, other than fleeing into the vault.

"What do you want to do?" she said.

"Passing traffic will give us some cover to get away," he said. "We can avoid a fight out front. And they won't want a fight immediately anyway."

"They'll want the money."

"And they need us alive to get the money."

Tracy avoided his eyes, but he was too preoccupied with the van to wonder why.

"Let's go back to the couch," he said. "Aaron's going to be done soon."

When they were seated, Raven said, "What did you want to ask me, Tracy?"

"What do you mean?"

"You asked if you could trust me. What was the next question?"

"Can I trust you?"

"With Aaron's best interest? Of course."

"What about the United States' best interest?"

Raven let a grin tug at his mouth. "You're not only his girlfriend, are you?"

"I'm actually his ex. On orders to give it a second go."

"Whose orders?"

"Does the name Christopher Fisher ring a bell?"

"You're from the Pickle Factory."

Tracy laughed. Her laugh echoed in the lobby but nobody noticed. The unusual nickname for the Central Intelligence Agency was a sure-fire way to talk shop without mentioning specifics.

"Yes, Raven. You know Fisher?"

"Very well. We get along most of the time."

"Aaron tried to hire mercenaries for this job but none wanted the work—" and she gave him a rundown of her conversation with Fisher. Raven listened without comment. When she finished, Tracy said, "But it looks like we're both in the dark. He hasn't told me anything you don't already know."

"Uh-huh."

"What do we do?"

"I knew something wasn't right. Now I'm certain. For now, we don't have a choice. There are bad guys waiting for us outside. We have to let this play out and get clear. It's the only way to know what Aaron's up to."

"Okay."

"And watch out for a fast one."

"You think he'll betray us?"

Uncertainty crossed Raven's face. "I don't know what to think anymore. I'm not sure Aaron is the same man I knew in the war."

TRACKING the Americans was an exercise in stress Fortun Dacourt never wanted to repeat.

Sergeant Bereau had followed through with tracing the rental car via road cameras. He had no doubt they were closing on Zurich and not altering their course. Dacourt boarded a private jet with Smoker and Sunglasses for a quick hop to Zurich.

In the city, they arranged a clandestine meeting with a group of cartel shooters. Using a map of Zurich where banks were highlighted, they assigned two shooters per bank, provided pictures of the male and female Americans, and ordered the crew to report if and when they showed up at any of the institutions.

The gun crew watching Bergstrom Brothers reported a positive sighting.

Now, as Sunglasses powered through traffic, Fortun Dacourt checked the load on his borrowed Beretta 92FS nine-millimeter. It was similar to Geneva's 93R, but without the three-round burst feature. Seeing the chambered cartridge, he stowed the weapon back under his coat. The Audi's engine growled from a burst of power as Sunglasses steered around a slow hybrid vehicle.

Smoker, as always in the passenger seat, held up his cell

phone. He'd plotted their course on the GPS app, and the blue dot representing their Audi was close to their destination.

"Two minutes," Smoker said.

Dacourt's heart rate picked up.

The shooters onsite in the van had orders to follow the Americans if they left before Dacourt, Sunglasses, and Smoker arrived. They needed the trio alive long enough to find out who put the money in the bank. Once the individual retrieved the cash, he'd get a bullet in the brain.

If his luck continued to hold, Dacourt felt confident he could greet the three Americans with more firepower than they had brought to the mall. Time to get even.

17

Aaron Osborne sat before Herr Bergstrom's desk. The banker typed information into his desktop computer. He wore a pair of small-framed glasses on the bridge of his nose as he worked, finalizing the account information before asking how much money Aaron wished to deposit.

Watching Bergstrom type and look down the center of his glasses gave Osborne time to think. Second thoughts about killing Raven and Tracy nagged at him.

He couldn't do it.

No way.

It was one thing to know what he had to do to keep his plans quiet. It was one thing to know his father insisted on tying off any loose ends. He had no problem killing those who were trying to kill him. But shooting friends in cold blood wasn't in his DNA. He had to keep them close for a while longer and figure out another solution.

He'd tell his father and Draco and let them deal with the problem. Draco had trigger-pullers who wouldn't hesitate. He'd still have to live with the decision, but at least he wouldn't be the one to carry out the killings. As if it made a difference. There was a lot riding on his venture. Should it go through as planned, he'd never have to work another day in his life.

War was big business.

Herr Bergstrom pressed a key and turned a bright smile on Osborne.

"I'm printing your documents now. One moment."

He left the desk to the printer set on a countertop to Osborne's left. Osborne let his eyes wander around the office. It was very drab, no windows. Lots of gray and blue. Paintings livened the place a little, but art wasn't Osborne's thing. The paintings looked nice, but he didn't understand their importance, or if they had any. For all he knew, Bergstrom had picked them up cheap at a yard sale. They might have no particular pedigree, weren't rare, and hadn't been created by any artist of note.

His hands were shaking. He balled them into fists to try and stop the shaking. Bergstrom dropped into his chair once again and presented him with papers to sign. While Osborne signed, Bergstrom inspected the cash in the briefcase. He called an assistant to help count the money. The assistant arrived pushing a cart with an automatic counter on top. The machine whirred and clicked as Bergstrom loaded each stack into the feeding tray and the cash cycled through.

"The exact amount stated," Bergstrom commented. Osborne signed the last sheet of paper. The banker gathered the papers, placed them into a folder, and offered his hand.

"Congratulations, Herr Osborne, we are happy to have assisted you today."

And almost as fast as it had been acquired, the money was safely out of his hands.

Bergstrom escorted Osborne, now holding the empty briefcase, back to the lobby where Raven and Tracy waited.

Raven thanked the banker for his help and the two

exchanged goodbyes. On the way to the door, Raven whispered to Osborne about the black van. The trio quickened their steps out the door to the Volkswagen.

"Drive, Sam," Osborne said, Raven already sliding behind the wheel. Osborne took the passenger side and Tracy the rear. Only Raven and Osborne buckled their seat belts. Tracy started working the catches to lower the back seat rest for access to the trunk.

Raven backed up and drove off.

"Van's following," Tracy said. She unlatched one side of the back seat, then the other, pulling it forward to reach into the compartment. She slid one Galil up front to Osborne, who immediately jerked back the charging handle.

Raven took his Galil and jammed it beside his right leg as he kept steady pressure on the gas pedal. Tracy passed spare magazines forward next.

Raven cleared one green light, traffic flowing without delay, but the next light turned red before they could get through.

"Still back there," Tracy said. She checked her own Galil.

Raven's pulse raced. He wasn't sure he could follow rule two.

"And probably calling for backup," Osborne said. He wiped sweat from his forehead and dried off his hand on his jeans.

The light turned green and traffic moved forward.

A motorway overpass lay ahead. Raven wondered if there was space beneath or beyond where they could make a stand without risking innocent people.

The whole scenario had all the markings of a disaster if they weren't careful.

DACOURT LURCHED to the left as the Audi made the final turn to pass the bank. The shooters in the blacked-out van advised their targets had left. If Dacourt missed them because of a few minutes' delay, he'd never forgive himself.

The crew in the van kept in touch via two-way radio while Sunglasses drove. They powered through traffic, speeding around cars, in and out of lanes, trying to catch up. The motorway overpass ahead served as a marker of sorts to Dacourt. He knew they were ahead, and hopefully they caught up before the Americans pulled an evasive maneuver to shake the van's tail.

Assuming they knew they were being followed to begin with.

Dacourt, as usual, needed a little luck.

The Beretta pistol weighed on his left side. Soon. Very soon he'd make use of the weapon.

OSBORNE SAID, "TAKING THE MOTORWAY?"

"We're faster and can get ahead of them," Raven said. "It's early enough there shouldn't be too much traffic."

The motorway overpass grew in size as they neared, Raven shifting to the right lane to catch the on-ramp.

"I think they know what we're planning," Tracy called out. "Getting closer. There's an Audi driving like hell and just pulled alongside the van."

"There's your backup, Aaron," Raven said.

Beneath the overpass was an open area of dirt, not big enough for a fight. Beyond lay a park with perfectly cut grass and lush green trees. And it looked empty. Raven changed lanes again, all the way to the left, and increased speed through the next intersection.

"Park?" Osborne said.

"Yup."

Tracy: "They're staying with us!"

"How many in the Audi?" Raven said.

"Three heads," Tracy said.

"How many in the van?"

"Who knows?" she said.

Three shooters plus...two? Three more? Were there more cars coming? Raven took a deep breath. He didn't like the odds. They might be facing more than they could handle.

"When we get out, shoot like mad," he said. "Get as many as you can before they exit the vehicles. Let's keep this short!"

Osborne said, "Read my mind, buddy."

Raven didn't bother to signal as he cut across opposing lanes. The front wheels hit the driveway of the park's small parking area. Raven hit the electronic emergency brake and spun the car in a classic bootlegger turn. The front now faced the road. Raven, Osborne and Tracy piled out. The van stopped at the curb and the Audi entered the driveway.

The Audi's tires screeched, the car turning 90-degrees to the VW's front. The doors opened. The three men inside jumped out with weapons ready.

Two more piled out of the van and ran toward the Audi.

Raven took a knee behind a bench, using the seat to brace his weapon as he eased back the trigger. The Galil bucked against his shoulder as the full-auto burst crackled. He shifted his aim, shooting at the two figures from the van, who were in the open. Both tumbled to the ground, rolling with their forward momentum, as the Galil's sizzling salvo sliced through them.

Two down.

Raven rolled left, dumping the empty magazine and reaching for one of the two spares in his back pocket. Slapping in a fresh mag, he zeroed on the three from the Audi, firing for effect, driving them to the ground.

"Tracy!" he shouted.

"On your right!"

Raven jumped to his feet and ran left to try and circle around the Audi's flank. He ran hard.

Tracy, flat on the grass, fired single shots as Raven made his mad dash. One of the shooters, who held a pistol, looked familiar, and Tracy finally recognized the man. *Dacourt!* The French drug pusher dodged between the Audi and VW, while his partners stayed in the fight. One aimed at Tracy, the other at Osborne, somewhere off to her right. She fired twice. Missed. The drug thug took a knee to return fire, Tracy rolling as the rounds split the air where she'd been. He wore a black suit and sunglasses and pivoted to follow her; the muzzle of his submachine gun focused like a camera.

Raven reached the Audi, dropping to one knee to shoot around the front bumper and keep his head from being a target. He triggered a burst that split open Sunglasses' back. The man with the chrome-framed shades flopped onto the ground.

The man between the VW and Audi swung a pistol around to Raven, and Raven raised his weapon to fire over the hood. The man jerked with the hits, falling hard against the front of the VW, leaving a smear of red as he tumbled to the ground.

One more.

OSBORNE REACHED the cover of a tree trunk and took in the battle before him.

He had a clear view of Tracy to his left, and if he aimed carefully, a nice shot at Raven's forehead.

Now! It would be so easy!

His finger twitched on the trigger as he aimed for Raven,

but he couldn't fire. He shifted his aim and triggered a burst at the last gunman, who was crouched by the driver's side of the Audi, trying to make himself look small. Osborne's rounds slammed into the center of the man's chest, and he slumped against the door.

Osborne wiped at his wet face, rising, trying to yell and breathe at the same time. He managed a curt, "Clear!" as he approached the vehicles.

He and Raven reached the VW at the same time, throwing their weapons into the back. Tracy reached the car as Raven started the engine once more. Raven surged forward, smashing into the Audi to move it out of the way. The Audi's tires screeched in protest, but the VW moved, bumping over the bodies on the ground, and then screamed toward the street and a sharp right turn back into traffic.

All three, gasping, said nothing as Raven made another sharp right, weaving around other cars.

"Nobody following us!" Tracy said.

"Anybody hurt?" Raven asked.

Tracy: "I'm okay!"

Osborne didn't reply as he sucked in deep breaths.

"Aaron?"

He shouted, "I'm fine! Get us out of here!"

Raven didn't need to be told twice.

FORTUN DACOURT FELT the heat of the VW's exhaust as the car plowed the Audi out of the way and sped for the exit. He felt a weight on his right leg, as if one of the VW's tires had rolled onto it, and he couldn't move the rest of his body either.

His wide eyes stared at the sky as he struggled to breathe. He didn't know how badly he was shot, but felt warm blood running from his chest to either side of him. The ground felt rough under his back.

As he struggled for more air, his vision began to fade.

If they had not lost the two shooters from the van right away, they might have had a better chance to kill the Americans. If the rest of the teams from the other banks had arrived in time, they'd have for sure overwhelmed the enemy. Forget the money. Revenge was more important. He'd failed at both tasks.

If he survived, he'd be in the custody of the Zurich police. If he died—well, his luck had finally run out.

Geneva, honey, he thought, and then his vision finally faded to black.

18

WITH THE PENTAGON REP FLYING ALL THE WAY OUT TO Nevada to see him, Mark Osborne, CEO of Osborne Defense, wasn't expecting a rejection of his latest bid.

But it happened.

"I'm sorry, Mark, it's not going to work this time."

Mark Osborne sat behind a big desk, with the uniformed Pentagon general before him. His home office contained several shades of gray, the usual couch and chairs off in a corner, small bar. General Ambrose didn't drink, so Osborne had not offered him any 20-year-old Scotch.

"What's the problem?" Osborne said.

Osborne Defense started as a company building planes for private and military use. Government work soon became the firm's bread and butter and they ceased serving civilian aviation. Osborne's big break came when he found a way to improve the fuel efficiency of jet engines. Osborne parlayed the deal into contracting to build explosives and missile gear. The contracts kept coming; his status grew; and now the Pentagon was telling him no thank you.

Over the last several years, his Missile and Fire Control

Division had provided the Navy, Air Force and Marines with Small Diameter Bombs (SDBs). These specialized weapons allowed fighter jets to carry a larger amount of more accurate destructive devices. The weapons gave two fighter bombers the ordnance of four, and allowed larger bombers to carry twice the usual payload. It had been a lucrative deal.

But contracts have conclusions. Osborne had submitted a new bid to continue the program, only to find competition from Boeing and other defense companies.

And now it looked like he'd lost.

"Boeing will provide the bombs a little cheaper."

"How much cheaper?"

"Enough to get approval."

"Jesus, Hal, are we talking pennies or big numbers?"

"About a billion less."

Osborne scoffed. "You buy cheap you'll get cheap."

General Ambrose tried to look sympathetic. He was a few years older than Osborne's 66, and Osborne wondered if he used dye to keep his hair brown. Osborne had enough gray to know the general's color had less than a 10% chance of being natural.

"Our new administration is a bit different," the man from the Pentagon said. "The president is tightening the purse strings. For now, we gotta go with Boeing."

"That's four billion bucks down the drain."

"How bad does it hurt?"

"It hurts enough, believe me."

Mark Osborne sat still. He felt like a football had hit him in the face, a stunned expression replacing the usual cockiness borne of late success and staying at the top of his game.

"I don't believe it," Osborne said.

"Try again in four years."

"You're sure there's nothing we can do?"

"I've tried. We've all tried. Your stuff works. The president doesn't see a need to continue with big spending on weapons when he's trying to keep us out of conflicts."

"He said that?"

"Exact words."

Osborne cursed. Companies like his depended on military spending. Maintaining a military to fight a two-front war was expensive, but more and more out of vogue with changing regional conflicts and the so-called "war on terror" which had no real front.

"Positive you don't want a drink?" Osborne said.

"Go ahead if you need one. I don't blame you. Actually, I'll take some water."

"Perrier?"

"Fine."

Osborne left his chair and crossed the room to the bar, poured some of his 20-year-old Scotch into a glass. He grabbed the general's Perrier and returned to his desk. Ambrose twisted off the cap as Osborne resumed his seat.

The general said nothing.

"You know me, General, I'm a patriot. We set up our bomb and missile program to make sure the United States maintains superiority anywhere in the world."

"Nobody's questioning you. We can't get the money to pay for it right now."

"It's insulting. It means when we do this again for the next contracts, I'm going to have to undercut myself."

Osborne swallowed more Scotch, and grimaced. He wasn't enjoying the drink or any calming effect. It tasted bitter and hit his stomach hard.

"Well," Osborne said, "I guess you can't win them all." He swallowed some Scotch and let the liquid burn down his throat once more. "You've never told me no before."

"This is one of those times," the general said. "I wanted to come out and tell you personally, considering—"

"I get it. I appreciate the visit. I suppose the president has no idea you spent tax money to come out here?" He grinned.

"There's a few other stops scheduled, so it's worthwhile."

"How much longer till you need to leave?"

"I have some time to mess around in your basement bowling alley, if it's okay."

Osborne smiled. "Let's go downstairs and get the lanes fired up."

Osborne downed his Scotch. Ambrose held onto his Perrier bottle as they left the office. They changed topics to their mutual obsession: football. Osborne forgot the grim nature of the visit as they began discussing the upcoming NFL draft.

MARK OSBORNE STOOD in the living room looking out at the front yard landscaping. He loved big green lawns, and he had one. Beyond, the desert stretched into infinity. His home outside Sparks was an oasis to be envied. At least he thought so.

"You were awfully quiet at dinner, Mark."

He turned. His wife passed him another glass of red wine. He took it.

"Disappointing day."

Brenda was in her late 50s; they'd been together for the last five years. She was the second Mrs. Mark Osborne. Breast cancer claimed the first. With his money and standing, he could have gone for a much younger woman. But with youth came a price he wasn't willing to pay. Brenda matched his maturity and understanding of the world, which was more important than a young trophy wife.

He drank some wine. The four previous glasses at dinner were starting to take effect, but they didn't take his mind off business. He found it strange so many people drank in excess 'to forget' while, for him, drinking did nothing of the sort. The booze seemed to amplify, more than anything, whatever problem occupied his mind.

"What else is on your mind tonight?"

"My son."

"He's been gone a while."

"What we're planning," he said, "takes time."

"He should be here soon, right?"

"Yes."

The telephone in the adjoining kitchen rang. Osborne still believed in landlines, especially being so far outside a city. If they ever required emergency help at the house, he didn't want to trust a flimsy cell signal. Brenda excused herself to answer. She yelled for him a moment later.

"It's Aaron!"

Osborne went to the kitchen, set his glass on the counter, and said hello to his son for the first time in a long time.

"We've landed in New York," Aaron reported after their greeting.

"What do you mean *we*?"

"They're still with me."

"Aaron, this wasn't—"

"You seriously want to talk about this now?"

Mark Osborne gripped the phone tightly, jaw clenched. Brenda saw the look. She shook her head. Osborne took a deep breath and let it out. He started counting, keeping his mouth shut as the numbers climbed in his head. It was a practice his father had taught him. *Always stop and count to ten when you're mad.* Osborne's response had been, *What if I need to count to 100?*

His father had told him not to be a smart ass, but added that Mark should take as long as he needed.

"You there, Pop?"

"We'll talk when you arrive."

The Osborne men said goodbye and the Elder hung up the phone.

"Need something stronger than wine?" Brenda suggested.

Osborne downed the rest of the red. "Yeah, I think so."

He was a realist. There was no sense in trying to tip over the chess board because you didn't like the moves you made. Aaron still had his friends with him. Not fine at all. But he had also secured the money to pay Draco's mercenaries. Mission accomplished. Now they could get to work on the next phase, but Aaron's friends were a complication they didn't need. Osborne would have a lot to explain to their partner if the plan went south.

Losing the SDB contract hurt, but Osborne always had a "cushion" built into his business plan to avoid long-term financial damage. There were billions of dollars to be made supplying the government with armament, yes. There were more billions to be made selling to allied countries. There were even *more* billions to make selling to people and places the US didn't want him selling to. Osborne's cushion included moving ordnance made in his factories, but unmarked, to whoever could meet his price. He worked through cut-outs to avoid detection, with connections all over the world.

Aaron was part of the latest venture to stoke a war between two countries itching for a fight but afraid to take the plunge. If the plan worked, Mark Osborne and another man named Orest Chumachenko would rake in a fortune selling weapons to both sides.

He hoped his kid hadn't screwed up anything by not getting rid of the dead weight.

So, yeah, he needed a stronger drink than red wine. After he finished the glass, he found a bottle of bourbon.

19

AARON OSBORNE DIDN'T SPRING FOR ANOTHER CHARTERED JET, and Raven didn't inquire why. He was thinking about what Tracy told him. The trio took a commercial flight from Zurich to New York City. Osborne and Tracy sat together in first class. Raven, having bought his ticket separately, sat in the rear of the first-class cabin. He wasn't acting as a lookout; he needed time alone to think.

Aaron and mercenaries and French drug dealers. Raven turned it over in his mind but found no way to fit the pieces together. Not by themselves, anyway. He was missing a crucial piece.

He examined each item by itself in relation to what Aaron had told him, knowing he'd told the same story to Tracy. What if he'd figured wrong? What if Aaron wasn't hiding anything after all? The pieces he had didn't fit a hidden agenda; they fit perfectly with the story Aaron told.

Could he be wrong? Could the CIA have miscalculated too?

He was flying to NYC with Aaron at his buddy's insistence. Aaron wanted to provide a proper stateside thank you.

There had been no reason for Raven to stay. Osborne even transferred Raven's cut of the stolen money to his account. For somebody with a secret agenda, Raven decided his behavior was all wrong.

But he still had his doubts. The only way to make sure was to stick with Aaron all the way to the end. If he was wrong, then Raven needed a break. If he'd reached the point where even old friends became suspects for no reason, especially one who had saved his life, he had to pause and re-evaluate. Had his war gone on long enough?

The jet landed at JFK where they hung out for the layover. Tracy and Aaron did some shopping while Raven bought a book and sat at the gate. They all wanted some space from each other, it seemed, and he was happy to oblige. Then they boarded another jet bound for Phoenix. From there, another change. Raven didn't dislike traveling, but the multiple legs of this journey were wearing thin. From Phoenix they finally switched to the last flight to Reno, Nevada.

By the time they landed at Reno-Tahoe International, Raven needed an Advil. His body was sore, he felt exhausted, and all he wanted was to fall into bed. Preferably alone.

They shared a taxi to the Peppermill Resort Spa Hotel. Osborne had booked rooms in the West Wing, the "budget friendly" section of the hotel. The rooms were located away from the main campus. Gotta keep the poor people away from the high rollers, right? Raven didn't mind. It was quiet. It was also a long walk from check-in to the West Wing. In his state of exhaustion, Raven would have liked a golf cart with which to finish the journey.

They had adjoining rooms. Osborne stopped Raven before they went inside. "Don't go too far. I'll call my father in the morning. If all goes well, you're invited to dinner. My father's wife is a heck of a good cook."

Raven unlocked his door. "I can't hear myself think so I'm hitting the sack. Good luck." He shut the door behind him.

Jet lag was the worst enemy he faced, and Raven tangled with the condition often. Two Tylenol PM helped with the aches and pains and made him pass out. He didn't wake till housekeeping knocked on the door a little after noon the next day. He'd forgotten to put out the Do Not Disturb sign. The embarrassed young woman, who didn't speak English, somehow understood his sleepy mumbling and departed. Raven tried to go back to sleep, but gave up after fifteen minutes.

Raven felt a little better anyway, which was nice after the night before. He showered and ordered breakfast. He could have asked for lunch, but he wanted an omelet stuffed with meat, and a side of buttered whole wheat toast. Per Aaron's suggestion to stay put, he did exactly as ordered. He had no desire to take another long walk to the main building. Venturing to the casino promised only an onslaught of noise and needless activity.

A knock at the door roused him from where he sat in a corner chair. He'd left the TV off and stared into space with his mind a blank for a change. He left the chair looking forward to his meal.

When he let the waiter inside, he frowned. The face was familiar, but it couldn't be the man Raven's brain told him it was.

"Yes, I am," the man said. "Your mind isn't playing tricks on you."

Raven blinked. Clark Wilson pushed the food cart into the room. Wilson was a Senior Staff Operations Officer for the CIA's Special Activities Center. He acted as Raven's point of contact whenever the Agency used him officially or unofficially.

"Shut the door and I'll explain, Sam."

Raven closed the door. A white tablecloth covered the top of the car and draped over all four sides. Wilson wore a white shirt, black vest, and black slacks—the uniform of hotel staff. A gold name badge with "Clark" emblazoned on the front completed the ensemble.

"The uniform fits," Raven said. "If your other job doesn't work out—"

"Haw haw," Wilson said. "The pants are too tight in the seat. If I bend over, I'm afraid they'll split."

"The glamour of undercover work."

Wilson set Raven's breakfast on the dresser. "You eat, I'll talk."

Raven didn't argue. He brought the food to the wall desk, lifted the lid, and attacked with fork and knife.

"Tracy is one of my people," Wilson said. He sat on the edge of the bed. "Fisher assigned her to this mission."

"She told me."

"How much did she tell you?"

"You're interested in Aaron because he was trying to hire mercenaries. But let's start from the top so I have everything."

"Tracy's control was in London. She and Osborne had a prior relationship, so we had her reconnect when he started behaving in ways we didn't like."

Raven took a bite of toast. "His spiel to me—"

"What did he tell you?"

Raven laughed. So much for eating while Clark did all the talking. He swallowed the bite. He told Clark the story of meeting Osborne in Paris. Wilson ignored Raven's report on the Paris terror attack.

"He told you he's almost broke?"

"Basically."

"Nuts. He was offering good money to the mercs he talked to."

Raven slowed his eating. His bad feeling had been correct, and he was about to find out how bad the true story really was.

"When we realized what he was doing, we needed to intervene," Wilson said. "His actions are going to make trouble for his old man's company, which we can't allow. Not with the top-secret stuff his father does."

"I told him the same thing. Let me get this straight. No mercs would take the job, he got desperate, and then conned me into helping with his 'poor me' bit."

"About sums it up."

"I don't understand. What's the money for if not to pay back his father?"

"We don't know."

Raven sighed in frustration. He wasn't getting the answers he wanted after all. Back to square one. But at least he wasn't alone in thinking Osborne had a secret agenda.

Wilson continued. "We sent Tracy to find out. He's been consistent with his story to her, and didn't tell you anything different."

"What if we're wrong, Clark?"

Wilson shrugged. "We have to make sure."

"What's the chatter in the French drug cartel? Are they still looking for him?"

"Yes. Fortun Dacourt is dead but his girlfriend, Geneva Ramsden, has taken up the cause. She's looking *hard*, too."

"I'd still like to know how they tracked us."

"Ask Tracy. She left the clues. Her idea was if the cartel eliminated Aaron, it would solve the problem."

"And get her and me killed too?"

"We figured you and her could handle yourselves."

"Fair enough." Raven wasn't about to get into an argument about the questionable actions of a spy agency. Operatives were expendable. Only the mission mattered. It was one of the reasons Raven had quit. It was the main reason he didn't go back. On his own, he wasn't forced to make such decisions. For him, people came first.

Raven ate more of his omelet. The chef had done well. The egg and meats complemented each other. But the conversation kept him from savoring the flavors.

Wilson said, "You're sure you didn't hear or see anything suspicious?"

"At a pit stop something upset him but he didn't say what. And with you here, and Tracy here, I don't get the feeling you're passing this on to the FBI."

"I can't pull Tracy out yet. I'm hoping you're open to snooping around some more."

"I've been doing so since Paris. I'll stay with it, sure."

"Can you get a look at his phone and send us the numbers he called? His phone record might tell us something."

"No promises, but I can try. I haven't charged mine so maybe he'll let me use his to make a call. Tracy might be a better choice, though. Can't you hack the phone?"

"It's illegal," Wilson said. "I shouldn't even be here in Reno."

"Fine. I'll break the law for you. If nothing else, we can find out who his bookie is."

Wilson laughed without humor. "His father," the CIA man said, "lost a bid the other day. If and when you meet him, he may not be too perky."

"Is the defense firm in financial trouble?"

"No, he still has active contracts, but the loss had to hurt him a little."

Raven's phone rang.

20

RAVEN LEFT THE DESK TO PICK UP HIS PHONE FROM THE nightstand. It was Aaron. Raven answered. The call was short. Raven listened, agreed to a time, and hung up. He said to Wilson, "I'm invited to dinner at the family's home."

"Aaron talked to his father?"

"He said everything was fine between them and we're doing dinner." Raven returned to the desk. He picked at his omelet a moment. "This might be a whole lot of nothing, Clark."

"At least you'll get a good meal out of it."

Raven scoffed. "After the last few days—"

"Between you and Tracy, we have the bases covered. And just in case, I brought some toys."

Wilson lifted one side of the cart's tablecloth. Two black cases sat on the bottom shelf. Wilson hefted the heavy cases onto the bed.

He opened the first and presented Raven with a bullet-proof vest.

"Think I'll need it?" Raven said.

"Won't hurt."

The second case contained a disassembled sub-machine gun smelling of fresh oil. Raven whistled. The weapon was a Heckler & Koch UMP in .45-caliber.

"I made sure to get something compatible with your pistol ammo," Wilson said.

Raven checked the parts of the HK, quickly assumed the gun, and announced his approval.

"I hope you don't need it," Wilson said.

"Me too." Raven put the HK back in the case.

AARON OSBORNE LEFT Tracy in their West Wing hotel room and made the walk to the casino. He needed privacy for a phone call. He'd waited until she fell asleep the night before to get on his computer. It only took a few minutes to transfer the stolen money from his Swiss account to another account where Draco had access.

He felt out of place as he wandered. Gone was the haze of cigarette smoke once so prevalent in Nevada casinos. "No Smoking" signs hung everywhere. The policy hadn't turned away business. Players packed the slot machines. One element which hadn't changed was the large number of seniors pulling on the one-armed bandits. They were a casino staple and always would be.

Security guards at the elevators asked to see room key cards before allowing access. Another change. It was an effort to keep prostitutes out of the building. Hooking might be legal in Nevada, but businesses no longer had to tolerate the activity. Osborne figured the policy wasn't about being family friendly. If anybody hiring a prostitute became a robbery victim, the hotel didn't want the blame.

The gaudy flashing lights, ridiculous bells and electronic noises drowned out quiet thoughts. Osborne hadn't ever intended to come back to Reno once he left, and the casino represented why. If he never heard another jackpot bell as long as he lived, he'd consider his life well spent.

At the end of a hallway off the casino floor, he found a corner near an empty conference room. He took out his phone and dialed Draco.

"How was your flight?" the mercenary said.

"Long," Osborne said. "I transferred your money last night."

"Yes. Thank you."

"We're having dinner with my father and his wife tonight."

"You'll get the building codes?"

"Yes. As soon as I have them your people can start."

"Do not fail us."

"Impossible. Everything is going according to plan."

"Except for your friends."

"I'll need help with them, and I have an idea."

Draco listened while Osborne explained his plan.

"Fair enough. I can spare a man," Draco told him.

"Good. Make it quick."

"Do your job, we'll do ours."

"Count on it." Osborne hung up and called his father.

"You got the money?" the Elder Osborne said.

"I transferred it to Draco," Aaron said. "He and his people are paid."

"Good."

"It won't trace back to you in any way."

"But I'm afraid it might snare you, son."

"I have a plan to make sure it won't and we'll get rid of Tracy and Sam too."

"Don't tell me. They'll join us tonight?"

"Yeah. We gotta make the act look good."

"There will be tears of joy. I'll get you the building codes and we're done with this."

"At least the first phase."

"One step at a time. See you tonight."

Aaron said goodbye and ended the call. He started back the way he'd come, back through the noise and flashing lights. The warm afternoon and daytime sounds were a welcome alternative to inside. He walked at a quick pace to the West Wing.

He hated to do away with Tracy and Raven but there was no other way. He needed them out of the picture if he was to make a clean break.

His pop would have trouble with the government once they found out about the security breach. His old man had his own plan to handle the questions. The initial idea might have been Aaron's, but his father refined the plan into an actionable set of goals.

Aaron was only doing what papa wanted.

Turning down Raven's offer of money, and Raven's continued insistence on the offer, drove him mad. He should have counted on Raven's generosity. But borrowing the money created a bigger loose end than bringing Raven into the job already had. Raven had friends, too. What he said about the cartel went double for them. If any of his allies found out what Aaron had done, he'd be a marked man. Much like he was now, thanks to the failure in Marseille, but while he might be able to stay ahead of the French cartel, Raven's buddies were a different story. Why be hunted from two sides when one was enough to deal with?

Taking the money from Dacourt and Ramsden had been the best idea. Nothing to connect with anybody else, a quick and clean theft, and considering how it had gone down, perhaps Raven had been right all along. But it still beat a source of funds the FBI and CIA might track. Aaron knew how they worked. He'd been one of them long enough.

He only hoped his equal insistence of turning down Raven's offer didn't make his friend suspicious. He didn't see how it could not have, however. At least Raven wasn't asking too many questions, or pressing the issue—any longer. He seemed to have accepted Aaron's reasoning, and Aaron was fine with the result. Now all he had to do was get rid of Raven, and keep his fingerprints off the killing to avoid a revenge hit. Having Draco's man do the job would keep him from being blamed. Perhaps not being willing to kill Raven himself was Aaron's subconscious working through the potential danger; he didn't care to dwell on the thought, though, because he wasn't sure it was true. What *was* true was he couldn't bring himself to pull the trigger, and the task needed somebody who wouldn't think twice. Draco was willing to provide the solution. The problem would soon be cleared off the table.

21

OSBORNE ASKED RAVEN TO DRIVE THE RENTAL TO HIS FAMILY'S place. Raven didn't ask why Aaron's rich old man wasn't sending a car.

Raven drove while Aaron and Tracy shared the back seat. Osborne looked nervous, almost pale with worry. He'd tied a bandanna around his forehead and it was already damp. Tracy watched him with an expression of care and concern. Raven shook his head. *She is one hell of an actress.*

"You okay?" she said to Aaron.

"I haven't seen my father in—I can't remember. Too long. We didn't even trade birthday or Christmas cards the whole time I was gone."

Raven watched the road as he drove but stole a glance at Osborne in the rearview mirror every few seconds. He genuinely appeared distraught. As if he expected his old man to invite him over only to throw him out as soon as he stepped through the door.

Raven said, "It'll be fine, Aaron."

"I can face a ton of guys who want to kill me but this is too much."

"How did it go on the phone?"

Osborne hesitated. Tracy gave him an encouraging pat on the leg. "It was a little strained at first, but then I told him I was sorry and it broke the ice. Then it as like all was forgiven."

"You tell him about the money?"

"He says he doesn't care but I'm sure he'll take it once his wife gets involved in the conversation. Don't tell him how we got it."

"Don't think he'd be thrilled with the idea?"

"Come on, Sam. I'd like him to believe for once I'm not a total failure."

He's either laying it on thick or telling the truth. Raven once again did not know what to believe. He chose to change the subject.

"Am I going the right way? You're supposed to be navigating."

"Pick up the freeway on-ramp on the right. The 445. After this light."

Raven caught the ramp as directed and moved into the middle lane of the freeway.

The elder Osborne and his second wife lived outside Sparks, a small town adjacent to Reno. Raven recognized the small town as a satellite of its bigger brother. More suburban homes and apartment buildings than big casinos. The usual shopping centers and chain restaurants. Raven figured the only slot machine action was in the gas stations and restaurants.

Raven's eyes itched and his throat felt dry. The desert climate didn't agree with him. He reminded himself to drink plenty of water before dinner to alleviate the issue.

Open desert on the left; more city sprawl on the right. They were heading for the Osborne spread in Spanish Springs. The city lessened as they continued on the 445, but then the big spreads began. No longer did they see single-family dwellings. Sprawling estates two and three times the size of regular homes took over the landscape. Osborne finally directed him off the freeway to a long stretch of two-laned road. They had only one destination. The Osborne family estate loomed at the very end.

Tracy said, "Did you grow up here?"

"Yeah."

"Must have been nice."

"My father put in a tennis court and a basement bowling lane but no pool. All my friends had smaller houses, but they all had pools."

"How come no pool for you?"

"My father hates the smell of chlorine."

Raven said, "Who doesn't?"

"On a hot friggin' day, who cares? You want a pool. Cheap bastard always had an excuse. Not like we didn't have room to spare."

Raven reached the end of the road. He slowed to turn left through an open gate. The single-level home resembled a crescent with a concrete center yard and circular driveway. Palm trees ringed the back of the house, with a few stray cacti hanging around like unarmed sentries. White stucco walls and a reddish-brown roof. It fit with the desert terrain.

Raven shut off the car. He glanced at Osborne in the rearview again. "You ready?"

A nervous nod. Osborne opened his door and stepped out. Tracy followed. By the time Raven exited, the front door had opened and Mark Osborne stared at his son like a man discovering water in the desert after three dry days. It was an appropriate analogy. Aaron paused midway to the front steps. He held his arms at his sides and stared back. Raven and Tracy moved out of the way.

"Aaron."

"Hi, Dad."

"You're looking—"

Papa Osborne didn't get to finish. As he choked on his next words, Aaron let out a sob too, and father and son met to warmly embrace. They held the pose a long time without words. Their tight squeeze and quiet sobs communicated everything either needed to say.

Raven turned to Tracy. She wiped a tear form her left eye.

Hell of an actress.

Or she really believes him.

Father and son finally separated, and Osborne the Elder said, "Welcome home."

"Thanks, Dad." Aaron smiled and introduced his father to Raven and Tracy. Mark shook Raven's hand and offered Tracy a hug, which she accepted. He said to Raven, "I hear you and Aaron are war buddies."

"Yeah."

"Thanks for looking out for him."

"He saved my bacon once. He's a good Marine."

"We can talk war stories later. Brenda has a tri-tip cooking and it smells wonderful. We got plenty of beer and wine too."

Tracy said, "I like wine."

"Then let's go and open a bottle," Mark said. "Tonight is a celebration. If you drink too much, we have a couple of guest rooms all set up."

Mark led them into the house.

22

INSIDE, THE HOUSE WAS AS NICE AS THE OUTSIDE. A MARBLE walkway lead down the center with a furnished living room on the left. The leather couches and glass coffee table sat on plush white carpet. Art decorated the walls, large paintings of exaggerated cityscapes. Raven figured each one came with a story and Mark would happily provide details if asked.

But now was not the time for a tour. Mark led them through the house to a set of sliding glass doors. They exited onto the back patio. *Yup*, Raven thought, *plenty of space for a pool.*

"Hi!"

Brenda Osborne stepped away from a large propane grill. The smoke from the grill carried the smell of juicy beef. She ran to Aaron first for an embrace, then asked who his friends were. As Aaron made the introductions, Mark handed Raven a bottle of cold beer and poured a glass of wine for Tracy. He gave Aaron a beer and Raven and Tracy exchanged hellos with Mrs. Osborne.

This can't be an act.

Raven and Tracy traded wary glances. He needed to talk

to her about the situation soon. He read only curiosity in her eyes.

Beyond the patio was Osborne's tennis court. On the other side of the tennis court the desert stretched for miles. Only jagged mountains stopped the expansion. The view was intoxicating. The comfortable evening temperature made Raven decide he could do worse than spend his final years in Nevada. *If I live long enough to retire.*

Brenda returned to the grill while Mark directed his son and his guests to a set table. Raven and Tracy sat next to one another while Mark sat beside his son. The bandanna around Aaron's forehead had dried. He wasn't sweating now, and Raven hadn't seen him this at ease since they started the scheme back in Paris.

Raven tasted his beer. He'd have preferred water, but he wasn't about to argue. Hydration was hydration. He wasn't a beer expert, but the brew was tasty. He looked at the label. Sierra Nevada. He chuckled.

Mark Osborne kept the conversation light. Brenda cooked and refused any help from Raven and Tracy, who wanted to let the Osborne men have their moment. They sat at the table and tried not to feel awkward as Osborne and Son talked.

Raven again wanted to revise his suspicions. Aaron had to have been telling the truth despite his wild operations in Marseille. Clark Wilson and the CIA were wrong. He was wrong, too. Tracy would have to come up with a reason to dump Aaron (again), return to Langley and continue with future missions. They'd need to handle the issue of the French cartel with direct force; one thing at a time, Raven decided.

Raven swallowed more beer and watched Mark Osborne talk with his son.

"What do you want to do now, Aaron?"

"Good question. I'm not sure myself. I don't think I could go back to the firm—"

"Why not?"

"Just isn't me, Dad."

"With your experience overseas, you'd be a great help to our sales department. You'd be on the road, not stuck in an office. You could talk to the military about how things really work in the field. I'll tell ya—some of the older brass seem to have forgotten what the frontline soldier goes through."

"I'd rather do something not related to war."

"Like what?" the Elder Osborne said.

"Like a bait shop. Something—"

"You'll starve."

"Then I'll go to the coast. California or Washington have plenty—"

Brenda Osborne turned away from the grill to approach the table. "You can't leave right away. You just got here."

Aaron held up both hands. "Can we not talk about this right now? I don't want to work for the firm. We'll figure something out."

"All right," Mark said. "Let's enjoy the evening. I didn't mean to upset you. Tell me what you've been doing. The last few months, I mean."

Raven frowned. *Last few months?*

The elder Osborne's tense expression caught Raven's eye. If they'd been playing poker, Raven would know he was bluffing a hand. What did it mean? Had the man slipped in the middle of a calculated performance?

"Well," Aaron said, "it hasn't been easy." He related his frustration with recent mercenary contracts and guarding oil rigs in the Mediterranean. Mark Osborne listened without interruption. When Aaron finished, he said, "Is being broke why you decided to come home?"

"We've been fighting long enough, Dad."

"It was a silent fight."

"Still."

"It's not what either of us, deep down, wanted, and now we have a chance to put it right. I don't blame you for wanting to go. Every man needs to cut loose from his family to make his own way. I always knew you'd come home."

Aaron finally dropped the bomb Raven had been waiting for.

"I'm going to pay back the money you gave me."

"Absolutely not necessary, Aaron."

"But I have it already. We can transfer it from Zurich."

"I appreciate the offer but your money is no good here."

Aaron had no response. His stunned expression said enough. Raven dipped his head a little to hide a smile. *Told you so.*

During the silence, Brenda announced the food was ready.

Raven let out a sigh of relief. The conversation had been painful to watch. He'd advised Aaron of the futility of his plan. He'd been right about fathers and their children too, assuming what he witnessed between the two was genuine.

But the cartel was still looking for them.

Aaron had created more problems than he'd solved.

NOBODY WENT LIGHT WITH DINNER. They piled plates high with tri-tip, vegetables, and buttered corn on the cob. Everyone chewed quietly for ten minutes. Then Aaron said, "How's business, Dad?"

Mark wiped his mouth with a napkin. "We lost a contract to Boeing." He told the story of the Pentagon general's visit. "It's very upsetting. But it happens."

A light wind kicked up, bringing with it a chill as the sun

continued its descent behind the mountains. Automatic lights snapped on to keep the patio out of the dark.

"It doesn't put your company in jeopardy, does it?" Raven said.

"No, but it will hurt the bottom line at the end of the year. We still have active contracts, but if the government's cost-cutting continues, the next set of bids when those contracts come up will be tough."

"You'll have to undercut yourself."

"Yes," the older Osborne said. "Then we'll feel pain."

"I always thought the words 'government' and 'cost-cutting' were mutually exclusive," Raven said.

"Maybe it's not the best description. They want to spend less money, but they still want their bombs."

"We seem to drop a lot of them in recent years, yeah."

"We have to defend America, Mr. Raven. I thought you'd understand the need."

"One of the reasons I work on my own now," Raven said, "is the so-called *need* to defend the United States and its allies became less of a need and more of a way for certain corporations to stay in the black while kicking back to the Feds. We fight wars for profit, not defense."

Mark Osborne's face went blank. Aaron stopped eating to glare across the table at Raven.

23

RAVEN IGNORED HIS OLD FRIEND. HE WANTED TO PRESS THE elder Osborne further. He was getting ideas again and didn't like the thoughts in his head one bit.

"You're talking about war profiteering, aren't you?" Mark Osborne said.

"If the shoe fits," Raven said. "I've seen too many bullshit reasons offered for why we drop bombs and send young men to fight and die for US policy. We get very little return on investment. Meanwhile the politicians get rich and stay in power and people like you build bigger houses and piss and moan about not being able to build more bombs."

"Hey, Sam—" Aaron said.

"I don't mean to be a jerk but it's a serious problem. We build bombs so we need an excuse to use them."

Mark Osborne held up a hand. "You're not entirely wrong. I promise you I do what I do to make sure people like you, Tracy, and my son have the means to defend yourselves."

"From fights we shouldn't be in to begin with."

"Then why do you—"

"I'm selective where I fight and when," Raven said. "There

are valid problems we need to solve and sometimes we need violence to solve them. But it amuses me policy makers ignore most of those valid issues in favor of battles where they have some sort of stake in the outcome."

Mark laughed. "For oil, you mean? We're keeping certain families in Texas rich?"

"Oil is a red herring," Raven said. "There's always another reason if you look deep enough. We don't ask questions if the war has been drummed up with false intelligence sold to the public to get their support. Appeal to patriotism. God and Country."

"I'm afraid there's a flaw in your premise, Mr. Raven."

"Who else do you sell to?"

"Excuse me?"

"Who *else* do you sell to?"

"I see. Well, we have contracts with several NATO nations and—"

"I have a real problem," Raven said, "with private corporations selling weapons to multiple countries. I'm sure you're on the up and up as you say, but your competitors might not have the same level of integrity."

"Selling to both sides of a conflict, you mean?"

"Exactly. Cashing in while thousands are killed for no particular reason."

"I'm sure it happens."

Raven spotted a reaction in the Elder Osborne's eyes. His face tightened like it had moments earlier. He stared at Raven as if encouraging further challenge. To continue would invite consequences, and none related to ruining a pleasant dinner on the patio as the Nevada desert cooled.

Wetness dotted Aaron's bandanna again. What wall had Raven cracked? If Aaron only broke out under stress, how much had to do with Raven's challenge to his father?

Raven shrugged and said, "I didn't mean to go off on a

rant. I've seen too much and it has made me ask questions nobody wants to hear."

"Questions are good," Mark said. "You've given me some things to think about. I will recommit to making sure Osborne Defense does the right thing. Even if it means selling my products for less."

Products. The word made Raven mad. The weapons of war were products resulting in broken young people sold a pack of lies in the guise of patriotism. And they weren't allowed to question their leaders. For the public, there was always a willing media and paid hacks to sell them the virtues of the latest never-ending conflict. The fighting only created more victims. People Raven sought to protect and often avenge. Their predators were those with money and power and the ability and desire to stoke the flames of conflagration and to hell with the mess they made. It never came to their doorstep. The blood of innocent people paid for their luxuries.

Conversation around the table ground to a halt. Nobody made eye contact with each other. Raven continued eating despite his now-cold dinner.

He felt eyes on him. He turned his head to the right, where Tracy sat. Something in her expression told him she'd detected the same look on the older man's face as he had. They'd discovered a clue to the Osborne agenda, but he still had no idea what their endgame might be.

Staying overnight wasn't an issue. Raven, Aaron and Tracy said goodbye after dessert and returned to the Peppermill. Aaron said little, and spent part of the drive fussing with his cell phone instead. Raven felt the tension. Aaron's face indicated simmering anger.

They split up at the West Wing and entered their separate rooms. Raven gave it a few minutes and then walked the distance to the hotel. He found the lobby office center where a computer gave him web access. He looked up Osborne Defense. Several news articles and press releases detailed their successes and developments. He looked up the company's manufacturing plant in Sparks. It was located outside the city near railroad tracks. Raven figured they shipped the *products* via train to various military depots around the country. Escorted convoys might also be on the list of options. Raven wasn't sure how the information helped or if it added anything to the jumble of unanswered questions.

What's the money for, Aaron? Your father said he doesn't want it.

Hijacking a train or one of the escorted convoys seemed out of the question. Both would have plenty of armed men standing by for such an event.

But raiding the plant might work. A crew only needed—

An inside man.

And a paid crew to pull off the theft.

What were you doing on the phone, Aaron?

Raven turned off the web browser and hurried back to his room. He needed to call Clark Wilson and get the big dogs working on his idea.

Raven closed the door and threw the locks and grabbed his cell from his shirt pocket. Before he hit Wilson's number somebody knocked on the door.

Through the peep hole he saw Tracy.

Alone.

Raven flipped the locks back and opened the door.

"Come in," he said, "and let's talk."

She didn't move. Now Raven saw what he'd missed through the peep hole. Tracy's face was pale.

"Raven—"

A bulky man with thick dark hair stepped into the alcove

and shoved Tracy forward. She crashed into Raven and they tumbled to the floor. Tracy rolled off as Raven scooted onto his back, trying to put distance between him and the big man, who stopped long enough to push the door shut.

24

RAVEN JUMPED TO HIS FEET AND CLAWED THE NIGHTHAWK Custom from under his jacket. He had no suppressor, and didn't want to discharge the gun. But the weapon served a dual purpose. As the big man closed on Raven, Raven swung the gun. The steel slide crashed into the big man's head and he dropped, out cold, on the carpet.

Raven pivoted to point the gun at Tracy's face.

"Whoa!" She put up her hands.

"Start talking."

"This man showed up after we split with you. Aaron handed me over and told him to make it quick. Then we came here. Clark and Fisher were right, they're up to something. This whole reunion was an act."

Raven lowered the .45. He told her what he'd found on the internet and his idea of Aaron acting as the inside man for a robbery of the plant.

"He stole the drug cartel money to pay his crew," Raven said.

"Do you think his father knows?"

Raven picked up his phone from where it fell. "I don't

know what else to think, Tracy." He dialed Clark. "You got a gun?"

She bent over the big man and dug a pistol and spare magazine from the man's belt. "I do now."

Raven told her about the HK and bulletproof vest under the bed. Wilson answered. Tracy dug out the gear. Raven talked fast and brought Wilson up to date.

"What's your plan?" Wilson said.

"We're going to the plant. I still have the keys to the rental."

"See if you can grab Aaron first."

Raven asked Tracy if she still had the key to their room. She pulled the key card from the back pocket of her jeans.

"We're on the way. Get whatever help you can muster and send it to the Osborne plant."

"On it." Wilson hung up.

Raven put his phone away. "Let's go see Aaron."

Tracy held up the HK. "How do I hide this?"

Raven told her to stash it under the big man's coat. He helped her pull the coat off the unconscious man. Raven's blow had cut the skin on the side of his head; a trickle of blood wound down his face. Tracy bundled up the submachine gun as if it were a baby and they hurried out of the room.

———————————

THE LOCK CLICKED and Raven entered first. He scanned the room with the .45 at arm's length. Tracy covered with the HK UMP. But the room was empty. Aaron had fled.

"Now what?" Tracy said.

"Let's get to the plant. Whatever Aaron has in mind is underway."

They found the rental car where they'd left it and Tracy used her phone to plot the route. Raven drove.

He still had no answers, but he expected to have the full picture soon. He drove with his hands tight on the wheel. He hadn't been wrong after all. Now he had to determine the scope of Aaron's treachery, and whether his father was involved too.

Raven turned off the rental's headlamps. One more block. The open space around the massive Osborne plant gave them a clear view of the complex.

The long building was brightly lit inside and out. The parking lot lamp posts also shined bright, but the field to the left looked dark. Raven slowed the car and pulled off the road.

He and Tracy left the rental and ran across open dirt until they faced the left side of the building. Light blazed in the rear, but they were flood lamps not attached to the structure. Somebody had set them up to provide illumination. Raven figured Aaron's theft of his father's ordnance was underway.

Neither spoke as they started forward again. They crossed the road, and stopped at the plant's perimeter fence. Another open field lay between the fence and the building.

"Did you bring wire cutters, Raven?"

"I can run to Ace if you want, or—"

"They didn't go in the front door, yeah."

Raven and Tracy traveled along the fence, scanning for threats. Raven. He hoped Clark Wilson brought the cavalry soon. But he couldn't sit and wait. Aaron had used him. He had more than a personal stake in the matter.

They followed the fence for fifteen yards. Raven spotted where somebody had cut the chain link. He pulled back one side for Tracy to slip through. He followed without getting caught on one of the clipped links. Tracy took a knee ahead to scan for danger. Raven joined her. She started to rise but Raven stopped her. "Look."

The shape he pointed out didn't fit the flat ground. It looked like a person stretched out. They approached and knelt beside the dead rent-a-cop. Somebody had shot him twice in the chest.

"He won't be the only one," Raven said. "Come on."

From Raven's review of the facility, they were on the west side of the building. The loading dock, where he'd seen the lights, was the north side, and faced the train tracks. As they neared the north side, Raven motioned for Tracy to stop and get down. Another fence blocked access to where the lighted activity took place. The combo of barbed and concertina wire, with its razor edges, made scaling the fence a losing proposition.

"We'll have to go through the front," Raven said.

They rose and altered course for the front of the building. Tracy stole a glance back. "Raven, down!"

Raven dropped prone in the dirt. Tracy landed beside him. He turned his body to look back. A Jeep rounded the back of the building. Two men aboard. They drove alongside the second fence at a slow speed. The man in the passenger seat held a portable spotlight. He probed the field with the bright beam of light.

"Are they expecting us?"

"Who cares?" Raven said. Any thought he had of abandoning the attempt to stop Aaron vanished from his mind. There was no turning back now. The raiding party had already murdered one innocent person. They wouldn't stop until they had everything they wanted.

25

RAVEN BRACED THE .45 IN BOTH HANDS. HE FIRED TWICE. THE spotlight winked out. The man holding it let out a scream cut off almost immediately by the second bullet.

Tracy fired the submachine gun. The windshield cracked, the driver's head snapping back. His body jerked as more rounds smacked into him. The passenger fell from his seat to the ground while the driver remained in place. The Jeep idled forward.

"Let's catch a ride," Raven said.

He sprinted for the Jeep, jumping onto the driver's side skid. Raven unbuckled the driver and let the body fall out. The driver was white, his face smeared with black cosmetics. Black fatigues and combat boots completed the ensemble of a man with bad intentions. A magazine pouch on his belt went with the M4 automatic carbine on the floor of the Jeep. The weapon sat between the front seats. Raven grabbed the mag pouch and driver's walkie-talkie. He found a key card to the building in the man's shirt pocket and tucked it in his own.

The hand-held radio bleeped.

"Kovalenko." A voice Raven didn't recognize came over the speaker. "What's the shooting?"

Tracy joined Raven as he pressed the Talk button to reply. "Where's Osborne?"

"Who is this?"

"Tell Aaron it's Sam Raven and we have business."

Raven dropped the radio on the ground and shot it to pieces with a blast from the .45.

"Raven."

He climbed behind the wheel. "What, Tracy?"

"How pissed off are you?"

"Enough."

"Enough to get us killed?"

"You can leave."

"I might," she said.

"What's your problem?"

"You know better than to go charging in there," she said. "We need to wait for Clark. If anything happens to me, the last thing we need is a dead CIA officer in this mess."

"You wait. I'm going."

"Raven—"

He stepped on the gas and the growl of the Jeep's engine drowned out her reply. He left her standing there. Hell with her. She could go and hide. He had work to do and nobody was going to stand in his way.

Raven's face showed a hard mask of fury as he headed for the front of the building. He stopped the Jeep at the lobby doors. The exterior was glass and steel framework. The lock clicked when he held the key card in front of a sensor. Raven opened the left-side door and moved inside with the M4 at shoulder level.

Empty reception desk ahead. To the left, a sitting area. A pair of double doors were at the far end of the lobby.

Raven cursed. Tracy had a point. The situation was

spiraling out of control and he was one man against an unknown number. He never should have gone this far. But he was too furious to listen to Tracy's reasoning. Rage blinded Raven because Aaron had betrayed his trust. He wanted to get even. And it was too late to retreat.

The double doors crashed open and a trio of gunmen stormed the lobby. Raven moved for cover and flattened on the tiled floor behind a couch. Bullets ripped into the fabric, stuffing flying. He fired around the side, a blind burst which burned through the magazine. The weapon locked open, empty. Raven traded the M4 for his pistol and fired in rapid succession. One gunman dropped. The Nighthawk flashed flame again. Second gunner down, his left knee splitting like a cracked egg. He smeared the floor with red. The third gunner slipped on the blood spill, crashing on his rear end. Another .45 slug opened his chest.

Raven put away his pistol and reloaded the M4 as he ran. He reached the knee-shot gunner and knelt beside him. "How many more?"

Pain etched the gunner's face as he struggled to break away.

"How many?"

The gunner reached for his side arm and Raven shot him through the neck.

Raven jerked his head up as two gunmen stopped in front of the lobby doors outside. They blasted the glass, shards spreading out in a puddle-like pattern. Raven rolled behind a wide support post. Bullets swarmed inside like angry hornets. Raven aimed around the post but only saw the backs of the gunmen as they retreated.

Raven ran to the reception desk and scanned the building map. He crossed the lobby to the double doors and pushed through. Long hallway with thin carpeting. Offices on the left, conference room and kitchen to the right. At the end of the hall a right turn into the warehouse. Raven's mind raced to grapple with how much opposition he faced. And when Clark Wilson might show with backup.

Gunners toting M4s rounded the corner ahead. Raven ducked for an open doorway on his left. He fired at the incoming gunners. Commotion behind him. The two shooters who'd shot out the lobby glass pushed through the double doors. Raven reversed his position and fired. Both gunmen fell in the doorway and blocked the doors from closing. Raven spun around again. He caught the incoming shooters in the open between the hallway walls. He squeezed the trigger and fired two short salvos. The shooters fell.

Raven ran forward. He stepped over the bodies and took the corner too fast but no threats met him. Through another swing door and he was in the warehouse.

The warehouse was huge. Concrete floor, only a few lights, the brightest light coming from the open sliding doors in the rear. Crates sat stacked in the open. More crates filled tall steel shelves which created aisles on the warehouse floor.

Raven went left. Feet shuffled in the maze of aisles. Raven froze and waited. Then he heard a voice he recognized.

"Is that you, Sam?"

Osborne!

26

An hour earlier, Aaron Osborne didn't say goodbye to Raven as he entered his hotel room. He and Tracy stepped into their room, and he slammed the door.

"That punk."

Tracy agreed. "What he said was uncalled for considering—"

"Shut up."

"Hey!"

"I'm done talking for the night."

"*Now* who's the punk?"

Osborne turned away. He didn't want to look at her. He wanted to be mad and his clenched jaw and slow breathing reflected his mood.

Raven hadn't simply been shooting off his mouth.

The bastard knew!

But how?

It wouldn't matter in another ten minutes. His father had texted him the building codes during the drive back. With Raven at the wheel and Tracy looking out the window, he'd forwarded the codes to Draco.

Draco texted back saying "a friend" would knock on the door as soon as they returned to their room. He was sending the "friend" to keep Raven and Tracy occupied until they completed the job at the plant. Aaron hadn't planned on built-in scapegoats; they provided a happy bonus. The FBI wouldn't look for him or Draco if they spent their time wondering why Raven had tried to steal US ordnance.

"Aaron."

He turned. She scowled at him with her arms folded.

"We're not done."

A knock at the door.

"Yes, we are," he said. He brushed past her to answer. Draco's friend entered. He was big and wore black. Osborne shut the door.

Tracy said, "Who the hell is this?"

"Take her. Make it quick."

The big man stepped forward and took hold of her left arm. Tracy, breathing hard, sweating now, shot wide-eyed looks between the two men.

"Get Raven next door. Do whatever Draco told you."

"Aaron—"

"Shut up!" Osborne raised a hand. She recoiled but couldn't move far because of the big man's iron grip. He didn't strike her. He jerked a thumb at the door and the big man dragged Tracy out of the room.

Osborne called Draco on his cell.

"Are they in custody?" Draco said.

"Yes. Where are you?"

"Waiting for you in the parking lot."

"On my way."

Osborne had no equipment to bring. Draco had everything he'd need. Without another look around the room, Osborne exited. He found Draco's black Suburban where the merc said it would be. He climbed into the back seat next to the man he'd met while guarding oil rigs.

Yakiv Draco had the typical Slavic "resting bitch face". He always appeared uninterested, bored, or mad. He was neither. He regarded Osborne without comment. The Ukrainian was shorter than Osborne, wiry, with a chiseled jaw and bony chin.

Osborne said, "What are we waiting for?"

Draco grunted an order at the driver. The driver put the Suburban in gear and left the parking lot.

"Where's my gear?" Osborne said.

"In the back."

"I'll change when we get there. Your men set?"

"They have breached the perimeter fence and dealt with security."

"Fine. Codes work?"

"Everything is satisfactory at this moment."

"You're a barrel of laughs, Draco."

"Your delay was not a welcome development."

"It's not my fault I couldn't get any mercs in Paris to sign up. Raven coming along was a lucky break. And stop complaining. We have him and Tracy to lay the blame on. We'll be across the world before the Feds begin to put the pieces together."

"We would have been successful without your friends."

"We'd still have Tracy to deal with," Osborne said.

"If you had followed my instructions in the beginning, you never would have taken up with her."

"I had needs. She was an ex willing to give it another go. What's the problem?"

"You Americans are always sloppy. You have no discipline."

"Draco, you won't get what you want without me, so I suggest you change your tone."

Draco said nothing more. Osborne scoffed. They had a plan to re-start a war currently on pause for cease fire talks. It wasn't business as usual; it was the war business. The best and most reliable profit center ever created. Raven had not been wrong. Whoever died in the crossfire didn't matter. As long as both sides kept killing, they would need tools with which to kill. Aaron's father made the tools. Aaron had to get the tools into the hands of the combatants and keep them coming back for more.

They rode the rest of the way to the plant in quiet contemplation. Osborne was about to change his life. Forever. There was no coming back from this. But the money he made would secure a nice lifestyle anywhere in the world. He had no particular love for the United States anyway. He could live wherever he wanted when they finished the job.

Stealing from his father's plant was a tactical necessity. The old man had supplied his cut outs with unmarked weapons before, but none currently had the bulk required to kick start the operation. The alternative was to take from the source, and Aaron knew where the crates containing scrubbed ordnance were. His father had set them aside purposefully for the theft. The plan was for his father to avoid suspicion by being a victim of a massive robbery. The old man and Chumachenko cooked up the idea themselves. Leaving Raven and Tracy to take the blame would keep the heat off until they accomplished their tasks. But after? Aaron had lingering doubts the charade would hold long-term, but his father had been doing illegal deals for a long time. He knew what he was doing. Or so Aaron hoped.

Aaron's responsibility was to not fail on his part of the mission. With Draco sitting beside him, and Draco's men already at the plant, he at least knew he wouldn't walk away empty-handed.

"Is that you, Sam?"

Raven bit off a curse and dropped behind a pair of crates.

The lights began winking out, plunging the warehouse into darkness. Raven stretched out on the cold floor to get his bearings and listen for movement.

Raven's eyes adjusted to the dark but it didn't help. The only advantage he had was the enemy was blind too.

Footsteps. Off to the left. Another to the right. He dared not waste ammo trying to hit targets he had no ability to see. He crawled around the crate and angled to the left. He swept his free hand in front of him. Nothing but cold floor and no obstructions.

Another step. Raven couldn't detect where the threats originated. He started breathing faster. *Steady.* He closed his eyes, counted to five. Where the hell was Clark Wilson and his backup? Raven finished counting. He decided to accept help might not be on the way. The only person able to even the odds now waited beyond the perimeter fence. Unless Aaron and his goons had already found Tracy. But Raven figured Aaron would gloat if he had. His silence indicated he didn't know where she was.

Easing to his feet, Raven heard more of the pounding of his pulse than any further footsteps. He felt along the corner of a crate, moved behind the crate to reach the wall. He kept his back to the wall as he inched left. Whispered voices reached him. Men getting closer. They thought they had him zeroed. If he could find a different place to be when they made their move, he might get the drop on some of them.

He moved a few more feet and bumped into a pipe attached to the wall. He felt along the pipe. It continued upward. He moved his back over the pipe and continued his slide.

A shuffle of feet, grunts. Raven dropped to a squat and stretched out on the floor again. A flashlight snapped on, bright in the darkness, illuminating his former position. The glare showed him parts of the two men who had hoped to find him there. Raven fired the M4. One of the men dropped, not the one with the flashlight. As the gunner with the light turned, he brought the beam online with Raven's new spot. The M4 cracked again. The gunman fell. The light hit the floor and spun. The beam came to rest pointing away from Raven. In its brief circuit, the light revealed a little of what lay beyond.

Raven jumped up, staying low, moving a little faster as voices yelled. When no answering call came back, somebody shouted for gunners to swarm the area and flush Raven out. Aaron's voice joined the shouted orders. He yelled, "I want him alive!"

RAVEN STOPPED AT A SHELF. HE FELT THE METAL EDGE WITH his free hand. He wanted a look in the crates for another weapon, a smoke grenade or two. He didn't want a conventional grenade with which to set off the entire stock. He moved forward. The voices and shuffling bootsteps had stopped. Raven had no doubt the enemy was closing fast, hungry sharks who smelled blood, eager for a kill.

Well, so was Raven. And he wanted the big fish in charge of the little fish too.

Raven reached the end of the shelf and felt around the corner. He eased to the right, peeked down the aisle. Who had owned the footsteps he'd heard from this side?

A scrape behind him.

Raven ducked and pivoted as a butt stock swished over his head. He stabbed forward with the muzzle of the M4 and met hard resistance as the barrel struck a man's abdomen. The gunner let out a cry of surprise. Raven jerked the trigger twice. The flash of flame from his M4 left a spot in his eyesight. The gunner collapsed without a sound. Raven fired another two rounds into the fallen man to make sure he stayed on the floor.

He turned up the aisle.

The flashlight blinded him. He screamed in surprise, trying to bring up his left arm to block the glare. Somebody grabbed his M4 and somebody else moved behind him to bash Raven on the back of the head.

As he fell, Raven's last thought was he couldn't tell which direction to turn for his next counter blow. He could not see anything.

THEY'D SWITCHED the back lights on again. Raven awoke from his forced nap. His head hurt. He retched a little but kept dinner down. Raven spat. He raised his head. Two men stood guard over him. They'd left him on the pavement. He looked up. Men in black fatigues hurried to load a box truck with wooden crates from the warehouse.

Aaron Osborne, dressed like the rest and with Raven's Nighthawk Custom .45 jammed in his belt, walked over. "He awake yet?"

One of the guards grunted in reply. Raven and Osborne made eye contact. Osborne dismissed the pair but told them to stay close.

Osborne knelt in front of Raven. Raven tried to sit up but his throbbing head made the move tough. He stayed on the ground. He managed to talk, though.

"What's it all about, Aaron?"

"It's a burning question, isn't it? Especially after all we went through to get to this point."

"So tell me."

"You had it almost right at dinner, bud. It's a bit more complicated, but you were close."

"I still don't understand. You did all this to rip off your father? You can buy guns and bombs on the black market. All you can carry. You didn't need to do this."

"You ran enough sting operations with the CIA to know only an idiot buys on the black market."

"Who are the weapons for?"

"Stop it. You weren't supposed to be killed at the hotel. You or Tracy. We *were* going to whack you here. Throw off the Feds. Where is Tracy, by the way? Can't have a clean getaway with her hanging around."

"I don't know where she is."

"You're lying."

"I'm not lying and you don't have time to torture me, Aaron."

"No, but one scapegoat is as good as two."

"She knows the truth, Aaron! The CIA put her with you after you started trying to hire mercs."

Aaron's face changed. His cockiness vanished; now he looked grim.

"Really? And you?"

"Wrong place, wrong time. Thought I was helping an old buddy who saved my life, and you roped me into your scheme."

"There would have been room for you, but you're always playing hero."

"Somebody has to."

Another sound. The noise grew louder by the second. Both Raven and Osborne froze, listening. The crew loading the truck didn't hear it, but realization dawned on Osborne same as Raven.

"Tracy must have called for backup," Raven said. He grinned. "Better think of something fast, pal."

Osborne grinned back. "Don't worry. I got me a warehouse full of hardware."

The noise finally reached its peak. Now the crew noticed. They looked up. A helicopter passed over the plant. A bright spotlight flashed on the loading activity. The chopper slowed to a hover. Over a loudspeaker a man said, *"This is the FBI. Stop what you're doing, lower your weapons—"*

The agent on board never finished his sentence. A shoulder-fired rocket flashed from the opposite side of the box truck. The chopper exploded. The orange flash lit the yard. Osborne didn't break eye-contact with Raven. The light from the blast lit one side of his face while casting a shadow on the other.

The wreckage of the chopper fell outside the yard gate, near the train tracks. The ground shook, the crash piercing in its loudness. Black smoke filled the air. More shouting now, beyond the fence behind Raven. Automatic weapons began firing. The cracks of the shots seemed too far away for Raven to place them. It didn't matter. He stayed focused on Aaron Osborne.

"Here's where it gets good, Sam. So long." Osborne took out the Nighthawk. He aimed at Raven's right eye. Raven didn't blink. He stared into the gaping hole of his own gun. The commotion around him faded. His only focus was the big black hole at the end of his gun. He didn't look at the man behind the gun, the man who once saved his life and was now going to kill him. Over what?

Osborne's face twitched. His trigger finger relaxed. He raised the pistol. Raven tried to brace for the impact but it made no difference. The barrel smashed into his head and the lights went out again.

RAVEN BLINKED.

"How does it feel to be alive?"

Raven let his senses return slowly. He wiggled his toes, felt life stirring in his legs. His head and face felt sore. He flexed his hands. Finally, he turned to the man who spoke.

Clark Wilson stood on the left side of the hospital bed. "You won't be here very long." Beside him stood Tracy Donahue. She tried to smile but the corners of her mouth dropped back into a flat line.

Raven shifted. He was propped upright on a bed, wearing a hospital gown. He gestured at the television hanging on the wall. "Does the TV have cable?"

"Why?"

"Might as well catch up on Downtown Abbey while I'm here."

"Sam—"

Raven let out a breath. "Feels like a truck hit my face and then backed over my head."

"He gave you a good whack," Wilson said.

"What happened after I checked out?"

"The FBI might as well have brought a knife to a gunfight for all the hardware they faced."

"Cut to the end."

"Osborne and his crew got away with two of the three trucks they'd loaded."

"Arrests?"

"Several."

"Anything to go on?"

"We can't wait for the Feds to share, especially since we weren't supposed to be there," Wilson said. "Tracy managed to get the phone numbers Osborne had on his cell, and we're hoping you might add something."

"I heard a name. Kovalenko. And Osborne said a few things before he hit me. About not trusting the black market."

"I'll check and see about that name. In the meantime—"

"I will be right here."

Wilson nodded and departed. Tracy stayed behind.

"Something to say?" Raven said.

"I should have stayed with you."

"He wanted us held captive until the break-in was over. Then they were going to kill us and leave our bodies. We'd take the blame for the break-in."

"Oh."

"And I should have known better than to go charging in like a rhino."

"But Aaron didn't kill you."

Raven nodded. "Cold feet maybe. Who knows? I'm not looking the other way. He and I need to settle this. Whatever he has in mind, I need to stop."

"We."

"Come along if Clark will let you. But don't tell the enemy where we're going."

"You know what I did in Zurich?"

"Clark told me."

"I thought it would be smart—"

"Save it," Raven snapped. "I had your job once. I get it. It's the spy business."

She nodded.

"It's what they do to us," he said. "It's why I got out."

"There are a lot of reason you got out, aren't there?"

Raven nodded. They said nothing a moment. Then: "You don't have to come with me, Tracy."

"I need to finish this, too. After putting up with his sweaty body on top of me—"

"Say no more. When I get out of here, let's go see Aaron's father again. What do you say?"

Finally, she smiled. "It's a date."

"Now scoot." Raven grabbed the TV remote from the nightstand. "I'm going to see if Downtown Abbey is on."

"Actually, it's—"

"A joke, Tracy." He winked. "Be grateful I'm not looking for Star Track."

She shook her head and left the room. Raven turned on the television.

28

RAVEN'S DOCTOR APPROVED HIS DISCHARGE TWO DAYS LATER.

Tracy picked him up from the hospital in another rental car. As she drove, he said, "What's the score?"

"Plenty. Clark has a full briefing prepared. We're going to Ukraine."

"Really?" Raven began sorting what he knew and tossed in speculation too. But he kept his thoughts to himself. For now. Ukraine meant a lot of things, but as he considered the current state of affairs between Russia and Ukraine, he figured his speculation wasn't far off.

Tracy continued, "We collected your clothes and things from the hotel. Clark put us in another one."

"I'll need another pistol."

"Don't worry."

"Aaron has my Nighthawk. I'm going to get it back."

"Of course."

"How are you doing?"

"I'm all right."

"You sure?"

"You know how it is."

"I do."

Surviving undercover work always astounded Raven. How one could become somebody else, do things they would not normally do, and go back to normal when the job was done, took more mental fortitude than ninety-nine percent of the world's population had. Normal was the wrong word, Raven decided. Nobody normal could turn on a new persona and then switch off. They were actors, trained to play a role, detach from their reality. They were better actors than anyone in Hollywood yet the only award they received was living to play another role. And hopefully living long enough to leave it all behind on their own terms.

Tracy's previous relationship with Aaron might have helped, but they'd broken up for a reason. She'd still had to pretend.

The spy business and the war business had much in common. Each left behind similar trails of destruction. Not everybody survived. Raven knew plenty who collapsed under the pressure.

Why he survived might only be known to the ghosts who pushed him through his war without end. He touched the locket under his shirt. He felt their reassurance. When they didn't need him anymore, he might find peace again. But for now, the next battle lay ahead.

He glanced at Tracy as she watched the road. She wasn't acting any longer. He looked forward to meeting the real Tracy Donahue. If she decided to reveal herself.

Tracy drove them to the Comfort Inn & Suites near the Reno airport. Raven still felt sore, but the doctor had said he didn't have a concussion. He'd have the bruises for a while. He was used to bruises and scars. The bruises went away but the scars remained, in more ways than one.

Tracy said Clark Wilson had secured three rooms, one of which was a large suite. Wilson was staying in the suite. It would be their home base until they departed. When Raven pressed her for more information, she told him to remain patient. Wilson had it all worked out.

"Are we sure Aaron is there?" Raven asked.

"If he isn't yet, the man he's working with is for sure."

Now she had Raven's attention even more.

Short elevator ride, down a hallway, and she tapped on the door of Wilson's suite. He answered and welcomed them inside. He and Raven shook hands. "Good to see you back on your feet."

"Tell me about Ukraine."

Wilson gestured to a dining table in the middle of the room. A laptop and photographs waited on the table.

He sat at the table and passed on Clark's offer for a drink. Tracy asked for bottled water. Raven glanced at some of the pictures but none of the people featured meant anything to him.

"Before Sam goes bughouse, let me fill in some gaps," Wilson said. He typed a password into his laptop. He asked Raven to sit closer. Raven moved over two chairs. Tracy remained in her place. She'd seen everything already.

Wilson turned the laptop so Raven had a good look at the screen. The CIA man opened the briefing. "The phone numbers Tracy pulled from Osborne's cell show he communicated often with two people. One is this man, whom we've identified as Yakiv Draco."

Raven examined the picture of the man with the bony chin and sharp jaw. "Never heard of him."

"You wouldn't have. There's been no reason for him to be on our radar, but he has a large resume. Veteran of the Ukraine military. When the Russians took Crimea and moved into Eastern Ukraine, he left the military to start his own militia."

"Why'd he leave the regular army?"

"Alleged war crimes. He hates the Russians and reportedly went out of bounds. He preferred fighting without official sanction from the government. As of two years ago, he's been working as a mercenary around the world. He left Ukraine because the Russians put a price on his head."

"How many of these militias are active in Ukraine?"

"Plenty. They're scattered all over, taking on the Russian ghost armies."

"The *what?*"

"The Russian ghost armies," Wilson continued, "are made up of contractors and foreign mercenaries paid for by Moscow. It allows them to maintain a presence and keep up the fighting. Moscow denies they're working under official orders, but they are.

"There's a cease fire right now," Wilson continued, "so the regular armies of both nations are on hold. The militias and the ghost armies are keeping the fighting going on a limited scale. Mostly they take pot shots at each other because both have limited ammunition and equipment."

Raven nodded. He added the information to what he'd speculated on the drive to the hotel.

Wilson changed the picture on the laptop screen. "Aaron also reached out to this man."

The screen showed an older man in a suit standing in front of a hotel. A doorman held the back door of a cab open for him.

"He's the Donald Trump of Crimea," Wilson said. "Big shot developer. He's overseeing the transformation of the city of Kerch into a tourist mecca for Moscow."

"Who is he?"

"Orest Chumachenko. Russian. Born in St. Petersburg."

"He's building a new playground for the oligarchs?"

"The real question," Wilson said instead, "is why Aaron Osborne is buddies with a Ukrainian militia leader and a Russian businessman. Considering Draco's background, if they're working together, I can't see them getting along well."

"I have a very scary idea," Raven said.

"Go ahead."

"You said there was a cease fire, but the militias and ghost armies are still engaged in hostilities."

"Right."

"Aaron is selling guns and weapons to both sides, Clark. Draco on one side, Chumachenko on the other. But they need a reason to re-ignite hostilities. The explosives they took from the Sparks plant are destined for a false flag of some sort. They'll hit a target important to Moscow, is my guess. Blame it on the Ukraine militias. Force the Russians to invade. Then Draco gets to kill all the Russians he wants and Chumachenko makes millions providing the guns and ordnance via the Osbornes."

"Think the old man is involved?"

"He'd have to be."

Wilson nodded. He grabbed a picture from the table. The photo showed the face of one of the dead men from the Jeep Raven hijacked at the plant.

"The dead man you heard the name of—Kovalenko. This is him. He was a member of Draco's militia. How they entered the country we have no idea."

"Ask the old man. There's your connection. He had to pave the way for the raiding party."

"Sounds like we need to talk to Mark."

"It will upset the FBI."

"Then let them get upset. We need answers."

Raven and Tracy agreed.

"Once you're done with Mark Osborne," Wilson said, "we need to get you two on a plane. We have no idea what the timetable is for this false flag, or whatever they have planned. The last thing we need is another wave of violence in Ukraine."

"Or a full-scale war," Raven said.

29

ALL RAVEN WANTED WAS A NAP. HE WAS EAGER TO GET
started after Aaron Osborne and his mercenary pals, but his
head and face still hurt. Advil helped but rest would help
more.

But when he stepped into his new hotel room, he froze.

"Hello, Mr. Raven."

The blonde-haired woman with pale skin sat by the
window. She spoke with a heavy French accent. He'd seen
her before. As Raven let out a slow exhale, he thought of how
she'd looked in the parking lot of a mall in Marseille after
being shot.

"Thought you could get away, didn't you?"

Raven didn't answer. He looked around, glanced in the
bathroom. She didn't have anybody else with her.

"I'm alone," she confirmed.

Finally, he faced her. "Are you?"

"I'm in your room alone. I have friends elsewhere with
Miss Tracy."

"I don't remember your name."

"Geneva. Like the city."

"Ah, yes. And your man—"

"Fortun. You killed him. Or one of your friends did. Tell me, where is Aaron Osborne?"

"I wish I knew."

"Don't kid me, Mr. Raven."

She wore jeans and a Tee-shirt with a light jacket. She reached into a pocket of the jacket and took out a small stainless-steel pistol. The sunlight through the window behind her, despite the closed drapes, glinted off the gun. She pointed the muzzle at Raven's belly.

"Don't make me ask you again. Lift your hands."

Raven brought his hands up a little. "I'm not armed."

She laughed.

"Aaron Osborne took my gun."

Another laugh. "The thief stole from his friends? Am I supposed to believe you?"

"You wouldn't believe me if I told you the truth. But, yes. Aaron took the money and tried to kill me. Or have his pals kill me."

"What pals?"

"The people he was working with. They needed the money for a job. Your money was untraceable."

"Sit on the bed."

Raven moved to the bed and sat on the edge. He still faced the woman. She brushed hair from her face.

"You're looking well," he said, "considering the last time I saw you."

"And you look a little rough."

"Compliments of our mutual enemy."

"Is he?"

"I'm looking for him same as you."

"Are you suggesting we pool our resources?"

"I flush him out, you make the kill?"

"And then kill you too? You have to understand—"

"I understand more than you think. But we can help each other. He's the one you want. The mall job was his idea."

"But it was your bank."

"Yes." Raven frowned. "How did you find me?"

"It wasn't hard. The mall cameras captured Osborne's face. We had to do more digging after Zurich. When we heard of two men getting involved in the terrorist attack in Paris—"

"Oh no."

"Oh, yes. CCTV footage gave us a nice shot of the two of you, Mr. Raven. From there it was a matter of tracking you or him down, and you aren't exactly unknown in some quarters."

"It's a risk I'm aware of," Raven said.

"Now you have run out of luck. Your reputation will finally bring your life to an end."

"But you need the money back."

"Osborne has it, you said?"

"You need me to find him, Geneva. I know things you don't."

She smiled. "Thank you for admitting the truth. Saves us a bit of time, doesn't it?"

From another jacket pocket she produced a phone. While she hit a number, her eyes and the muzzle of the autoloader never left Raven's face. Geneva said into the phone, "Do you have her?"

Tracy.

"Put her in the car and take her to the safe house. I have Raven. Send me two men to get him to the other car and we'll meet you."

She ended the call and put her phone away.

"You're going to tell us everything, Mr. Raven. And when you've said your last words, I'll shoot you myself."

"We'll see, Geneva."

THEY JAMMED Raven into the back seat of a sedan with Geneva on one side and a goon on the other. A second goon drove. Since she only spoke French to the two men, Raven figured they didn't understand English.

He had no weapon. They'd taken his phone too. No way to reach Clark. He wondered about Tracy. Was she hurt? If they hadn't injured him, yet, they might have held back with her too. The torture would come later, he figured. Raven had no doubt he'd need a solution before they started. Otherwise, there was no way out. They faced brutal cartel thugs. It made no difference if they were from Europe or south of the US border. When it came to violence and depravity, the cartels were in a league of their own, no matter where they came from.

They surprised him by not tying a blindfold over his eyes. He decided it didn't matter. He wasn't expected to leave alive. They followed the freeway out of town and presently pulled off to follow a two-lane road. Raven might have guessed they were driving to the Osborne estate, but it wasn't the same road. The driver continued along for another fifteen minutes. Their car was the only one present. The vehicle with Tracy must have already arrived at their destination.

Raven had seen Tracy in action. Her fighting ability wasn't in question, but they hadn't yet gelled as a team. What he hoped was she'd be already working on an exit plan same as he was. If they could follow each other's signals, they might have a chance.

Might.

And then Raven laughed to himself.

"What is so funny?" Geneva said.

"I told Aaron this would happen. Except it wasn't supposed to be me in the car."

They drove into the mountains following the twisty road. At the end they stopped at a cabin about as isolated as the Osborne house. There was another car in the garage already. When Geneva and her thugs pushed Raven out, he heard the engine of the second car ticking as it cooled. The crew who had grabbed Tracy hadn't been there for long.

Raven didn't get a chance to look outside. The goons shoved him forward. All he knew was they were well outside Reno. It was going to be a long way back.

Geneva split off for another room while the goons steered Raven down a hall. They shoved him into an empty bedroom. He tumbled onto the carpet. The door slammed shut behind him.

"Welcome to the jungle," Tracy said.

She sat in a corner against the wall. At least the carpet was soft. And brand new. Raven slowly rose to hands and knees. His head spun. "Where are we?"

"An unfinished cabin."

"If only they'd grabbed us when Aaron was still here. They might have spoiled his plant raid."

"Ifs and buts."

"Uh-huh." Raven stretched out on the floor. It felt good to finally lay down. A pillow would have been wonderful. He stared at the ceiling. "Guess we're in for it."

"Got a plan?"

"Working on one."

"I have no intention—"

"Me neither."

"I'm going to add this to Aaron's account," she said.

"Get in line," Raven told her.

"We should have killed both of them at the mall."

"Wouldn't have made any difference, Tracy. I told Aaron this was going to happen."

"Why did you help him?"

"He's a friend. He saved my life once."

"You still have your cut of the money?"

"Yes."

"Is it—"

"Part of my plan?" he said. "Bet your ass. But if you find an opening before me—"

"We will have no trouble coordinating, Raven."

"Call me Sam."

"No," she said.

30

Raven sat up and frowned at Tracy. "What's the problem?"

"I don't like getting too familiar with people."

Raven lay down again. She had her own Rule One (No Roots) same as he did. And why not? The mix of roles and personas she'd had to develop over the years, the danger and mistrust, made hyper-vigilance a natural byproduct. And those who were hyper-vigilant built walls to protect themselves. They never knew who might stab them in the back. When you didn't know friend from foe, you trusted nobody.

"Lousy way to live, Tracy. I don't like roots either but you can't close people out entirely."

"It's none of your business. I thought you of all people would appreciate keeping secrets."

"Clark knows my history," Raven said. "My past isn't a total secret."

"Whatever."

Before Raven said more, the door opened and four thugs entered. Two for each. The pair Raven had ridden with in the car grabbed him. The other two grabbed Tracy. Neither resisted. The goons marched them out of the room and down the hall. The group descended steps to a lower floor. More unfinished space at the end of the steps. A crisscross of wooden frames and ceiling beams, with only a few of the gaps filled with sheet rock, made up the space. On a folding table lay hand tools and a power drill.

The drill made Raven shiver. The Irish Republican Army had used drills to torture British agents. He'd have to work fast. Once Geneva started with the drill, game over.

The goons forced Raven and Tracy into metal folding chairs and they sat beside one another. The goons spread out but not too far. None of them made any move to tie Raven or Tracy. The pistols they wore on either belt or shoulder harness were deterrent enough. At least until they became an advantage. If Raven hustled fast enough.

Geneva finally joined them. She chuckled at the sight of Raven and Tracy seated and moved to the table with the tools.

"Where is Osborne?"

Raven said, "We think he's in Ukraine, or on his way."

"Why?"

"Not sure."

"Does he have my money?"

"Last I saw of the money was Zurich."

"Really?"

"I'll tell you the whole story if you want."

Geneva turned from the table, folded her arms, and said, "This I'd like to hear."

Raven began with how he met Osborne in Paris, how they planned to steal the drug money, and why.

Geneva laughed. "You're a sucker."

Raven shrugged. "He used our friendship against me."

To Tracy, the French woman said, "And you, darling?"

"Just a girl along for the ride," Tracy said.

"This is fascinating," Geneva said. She picked up the drill and held it in both hands. "It's almost too ridiculous to believe."

"I told you," Raven said, "we have a mutual interest here. Let's work together."

"I don't think so. You've admitted you're both idiots. What's the benefit to me?"

Raven blinked. He had to answer fast. Geneva was tapping the side of the drill with her trigger finger.

"We know his contact in Ukraine," Raven said.

"Tell me."

"Let's make a deal."

She snapped an order to two of the thugs who stepped to Tracy's chair and held her in place on either side. Tracy fought against their iron grip, then gave up. Her hot eyes watched Geneva.

Geneva went to Tracy and held the drill over her right knee. Tracy struggled some more. One goon held her head while the other knelt to control her midsection.

Geneva looked at Raven. "No deals, Mr. Raven."

The French woman pulled the trigger. The drill's shrill motor filled the room and the thin bit with its pointy end spun. Tracy screamed. Geneva laughed. She let go of the drill's trigger and the shrill noise faded.

"I don't want to get blood all over my jeans," Geneva said. "Tell me what I want to know, and I'll kill you both fast."

The goons let go of Tracy. She breathed hard. Sweat coated her face.

"I can give you part of the money," Raven said.

"What do you mean?"

"My cut. It's in my bank. In Zurich. Between the money and the name of Aaron's contact, we deserve—"

"You deserve *nothing*!" She lunged at Raven, switching the drill to her left hand. She slapped him with her right. The sting hurt and Raven's face twisted in pain. "You took from me the man I loved! This isn't *only* about money!"

Tracy shouted, "He played us! It was all Aaron's plan! We're nothing to you!"

Geneva pivoted to Tracy. "You're so right, darling. Hold her head while I drill out one of her eyes!"

Geneva took a step toward Tracy as the thugs resumed their grip. Tracy let out another scream barely overpowered by the whine of the drill.

Raven stuck his left leg out.

Geneva tripped. Worse, she fell forward with the drill screaming at full power and Raven knew there would be no better chance than now.

Geneva shuffled to correct her fall but gravity had her. Instead of plunging the spinning drill bit into Tracy, she collided with the thug holding Tracy's legs. The man tried to move but wasn't fast enough. Geneva smashed into her compatriot. The drill punctured his left arm, went deep, and his scream joined the chorus.

Raven jumped out of his chair, grabbed the back and swung at the thug coming at him. Metal struck skull and the thug checked out. Raven tossed the chair at the second nearest thug, who ducked. Raven dived for the one he clocked out as the other dug for his pistol. Raven rolled away as the thug fired, but in his hand was the unconscious goon's gun and he used it to good effect. He fired once and gave the gunman a third eye in the middle of his wide forehead.

Raven, still on the ground, swung the pistol in Tracy's direction.

The goon with the hole in his shoulder had a sheet of blood down his sleeve and on his shirt. He scrambled for the table, crying, yelling. Geneva was on hands and knees trying to get on her feet.

The last goon standing had Tracy out of her chair and

tried to pull her in front of him as a shield. Tracy stomped on one of his feet, smashed a bony elbow into his face. With a yell he wrapped an arm around her neck and held tight.

Raven shifted his aim and shot Geneva in her plump rear end. With a howl she stopped trying to get up and flopped on her belly.

The goon with the drilled shoulder reached the table and grabbed a wrench. He threw it at Raven, who let it fly by, and then aimed for the man's right nostril. He pulled the trigger and gave the goon a nine-millimeter nose job. The slug caved in his face as a bonus.

Tracy and the last goon continued their struggle, Tracy unable to break the man's arm from around her neck. But she scored another hit with an elbow strike. The man's nose was smashed and bleeding.

Raven swung the pistol around and Tracy jerked her head out of the way. Raven triggered another round and a chunk of the goon's jaw splattered on the sheet rock behind him. *Then* he let go, and as Tracy dived for the floor Raven fired a final time and the goon collapsed.

He turned his attention back to Geneva and her bleeding behind. She started to crawl toward the table. She moaned a lot.

"Nuts," Raven said. He stood and went to her, grabbed a shoulder and flipped her onto her back. Her face, a mix of pain and rage, jaw clenched, reflected only hate echoed by the fire in her dark eyes. Raven shot her in the head and then her eyes were as dead as the rest of her.

Tracy retrieved a pistol from the floor and said, "Nice one."

"Let's get out of here. Who's got the keys to one of the cars?"

It didn't take long to find the keys.

31

TRACY DROVE BACK TO THE HOTEL. IT WAS LATE IN THE DAY and Raven felt very tired after the fight. Tracy wondered if Clark was looking for them as she parked the car. Raven hadn't bothered to call since he figured she would. They laughed, then called him from the car. Wilson sounded relieved when he heard their voices.

"What went wrong?" the CIA man said.

Raven explained.

"Why couldn't they have shown up sooner?" Wilson said.

"I made the same joke," Raven told him.

"Get up to the suite. We need to go over the latest and it's no laughing matter. Sam, your theory is probably correct. Washington is shitting itself with the idea."

Tracy chimed in, "We need some time, Clark."

"You have thirty minutes." Wilson ended the call.

"Yay," she said as she put the phone away.

"I don't work for you guys anymore," Raven said, "so I can tell him to screw off."

Tracy exited the car and Raven followed. She said, "See

you in thirty minutes, Raven." He grinned but didn't argue. They went their separate ways back to their rooms.

Raven turned on the shower and tried to soap up but his hand shook. He leaned his head against the stall wall, let the hot water stab at him, and let himself shake. Geneva Ramsden's had been a close call he never saw coming, despite Wilson's earlier warning. He hadn't seen them watching him. He could never allow himself to slip again. Next time he might not be so lucky. With a deep breath he finally settled and finished his shower. He didn't go looking for food because he figured Clark would have something. What he did instead was lay down and doze for his last 15 minutes before the new briefing.

Clark anticipated their need for food and had a tray of hot sandwiches and drinks waiting. They sat around the dining table. Wilson referenced his open laptop and a large map of Crimea, also on the table, as he spoke.

"We're talking about a powder keg and it's going to explode," he said.

"The analysts think my false flag theory is good?" Raven said. He bit into a roast beef sandwich.

"Yes," Wilson said. "The short version is, Crimea is firmly under Russian control. After they annexed the peninsula in 2014, it started the war. It's officially a low-intensity conflict, but come on, war is war.

"In Crimea," Wilson said, "we have a split between Russian forces, Ukrainian nationalist rebels, and a citizenry who favors the Russians. The nationalists have been engaging in acts of sabotage since the annexation. Not a lot, two or three times a year, but they're making Moscow nervous. They've blown up power lines, Russian supply lines, and other small strikes. They want to make Crimea as tough to manage as they can so Russia gives up. The Russians usually respond with mass arrests looking for the instigators."

"Some things never change," Raven said.

"The power station bombings caused a lot of problems, and Moscow sent more troops. There are now close to ten thousand Russian soldiers in Crimea. They back up local authorities."

Tracy jumped in. "The Nationalists make the perfect group to frame for a false flag."

"Exactly."

"Do we have an idea of their target?"

"It's a big one." Wilson drew a circle on the map. The circle was in the middle of a short gap between Russia and Crimea, the Kerch Straight. "Here is the Crimean Bridge," he said. "Links the two countries. It was a big deal for the Russians to build it, and the Ukrainians did everything they could to stop them. They failed. If anything happened to this bridge, Moscow would respond with force. No doubt in anybody's mind."

"They have the explosives to do the job, too," Raven said. "What does the president think of this?"

"He's already talking to Moscow. Also, the secretary of state is hosting a video conference between Russian and Ukrainian reps to see if we can't get some cooperation. There's too much ground to cover. Your primary job is to get Aaron Osborne, and we don't care if he's dead or alive. We want the bombing stopped too, but we can't expect you two to do everything."

"Will we have any help?" Tracy twisted off the cap of a bottle of water and drank.

"We don't have anybody in Crimea at the moment. Our personnel are at the embassy in Kiev. They can monitor from afar, but no, you two are it. We have journalist cover identities worked out."

Raven said, "What about Aaron's cell phone? Any activity on it?"

Wilson shook his head. "Not yet. He may have ditched it."

"Chumachenko can lead us to him," Tracy said, "if all else fails."

"Remember Chumachenko is a major public figure, has friends in the Kremlin, and won't be a cinch."

"Clark, come on. It's me." Raven grinned.

"Wipe the mustard off your lip, tough guy," Tracy said.

Wilson laughed. Raven sheepishly used his napkin.

"Chumachenko has an office in Kerch, and a big house outside the city," Wilson said. "I'll send the details to your phones."

"When do we leave?" Tracy said.

"Tomorrow morning. From here to JFK, then Air France to Paris, where you'll pick up your Crimean connection. Enjoy fourteen hours of blissful air travel."

"If we're reporters," Raven said, "did our 'network' spring for first-class seats?"

"Sorry, Sam, you two work for an obscure blog nobody reads. Cheap seats all the way."

"How nice of our uncle," Raven said. He nudged Tracy. "This is another reason I quit."

"Gee, Sam, I see so much of you lately it's like you still work for us," Wilson said.

"Well, next time, I won't have anything to do with you, watch. You won't have any fun without me."

"All right, both of you get out of here," the CIA man said. "Get some sleep. It's going to be a long trip."

Raven and Tracy headed for the door. Raven asked for an update as soon as Wilson heard about the secretary of state's video conference. Wilson assured him he would.

"I'm not holding my breath, though," Raven said. "The

Russians will want to keep Ukraine out and do everything themselves."

"Like you said, Sam," Wilson said, "things never change."

32

AARON OSBORNE GROANED AS HIS STOMACH LURCHED FOR THE umpteenth time. The ocean wasn't being kind. The rough sea beat hard on the freighter's hull, and Aaron seemed to be the only one affected. Or he was the only member of the team showing his discomfort. Draco and the Ukrainian mercenaries were a tough lot.

He moved along the corridor from the head back to his cabin. Draco approached from the other end. He blocked Aaron's path in the narrow space.

"Never get used to the ocean, do you?"

"At least the oil rigs didn't move," Aaron said. "And I always found a way to avoid duty in the patrol boats, remember?"

"One of the others might need some of your seasick pills."

"For all the good they do me. I thought you all had guts of iron."

"Arkady is being very tough, but if he keeps turning purple like he has, he'll soon resemble a radish."

"He can come by any time, or I'll slip him a few when nobody's looking."

"Very good."

Draco stepped aside and Aaron continued on. When he reached his cabin, he locked the door and rolled onto an army cot. Their accommodations weren't five-star worthy, but he didn't care. Fluorescent lights blazed above. He covered his eyes with his right forearm.

Going to Kerch by sea hadn't been his idea. Chumachenko controlled the section of the waterfront where they planned to dock. He said it was the most efficient way, and he was also the boss since they were now outside the United States. Aaron's only reply had been "Yes, sir." But he didn't like the down time. Too much could happen; actually, go wrong; in the time it took to complete the voyage.

And any of those problems would be his fault.

Raven and Tracy were still alive. While he should have stuck to the plan to get rid of them, the fact was he couldn't.

There were consequences to his failure. He knew Raven wouldn't give up the chase. It wasn't in his DNA to quit. Aaron had used Raven when he needed him, knowing the risks. The reward had outweighed the risks, or so he thought at the time.

Draco was already displeased. Chumachenko was likely furious too. Aaron knew Draco had updated the boss before their departure.

And what of his father? Raven could testify to Aaron's involvement. The feds might consider his father a victim. Maybe not. How long could his father hold up under the scrutiny? Had Aaron jeopardized his father's future business with the government, and thereby the entire scheme, by failing to leave Raven's body behind?

Too many questions with no answers.

And a long way to go before they reached Kerch.

Aaron began to wonder if he'd survive long enough to see his financial goals to fruition.

He had Raven on his trail.

He knew Chumachenko was not one to tolerate failure.

But there was no turning back now.

DRACO LEFT the head but didn't return to his cabin. He went up top, port side, to watch the choppy ocean. The cold wind felt good.

He gazed at the horizon. Ocean surrounded them on all sides. Not a hint of land anywhere. The water carried with it Draco's conflicting thoughts.

He had left Ukraine for the mercenary world after the initial cease fire. His militia, near broke, had to scrape for every bullet and bomb they could find. Their harassment of ghost army camps did nothing to chase the invaders from his land. Nor did the fighting bring any solace to Draco. The Russians had taken everything from him; he wanted to make them hurt. Pot shots in the middle of the night didn't make them hurt enough.

During the heaviest fighting after the annexation, Draco had been a soldier in the 13th Army of Ukraine. They'd fought boldly against the invaders. Both sides soon found themselves stalemated as the diplomats took over. The government investigation into Draco's alleged war crimes would for sure land him in prison, or worse. He was very guilty, and didn't feel shame. But conviction would take him out of the fight for good. He quit the army and formed his own militia. When his private war reached an impasse of its own, and the government investigation determined his guilt, he took off.

The Russians had killed his family. Wife, two children. Gone in an instant. He killed every Russian he found to avenge them. The blood lust did nothing but send his own government after his neck.

He met Aaron Osborne on an oil rig in the Mediterranean. They forged a connection as only two men on guard duty in the middle of nowhere could. He didn't consider Aaron a friend. Somebody like Draco had no friends. All Draco lived for was war. Aaron seized on Draco's desire to return home and beat the Russians for good. What if somebody, an outsider, could supply the arms and munitions required to bring the fighting to an end? Bring victory to Ukraine? Draco liked the idea too.

Aaron's initial meetings with his father, mostly spent repairing their relationship, didn't move the project forward at first. But between the two of them, they convinced the Elder Osborne to begin the project. Mark Osborne reached out to other connections around the world, and arranged a meeting with Orest Chumachenko. The Russian businessman already had a side business supplying arms to the ghost armies, but the need for discretion limited his reach. What he needed was an outside supply, and Mark Osborne offered such a supply.

Draco did not like the idea of working with Chumachenko. The man was a Russian, and one of the worst. A two-faced snake with his own agenda. But Draco was also pragmatic. If conspiring with a Russian enabled him to kill more Russians, then it would be easy, in the midst of the fighting, to pop Chumachenko between the eyes. Draco could tolerate the man as long as he knew, in the back of his mind, he'd soon bring the big shot to his end.

With the freighter loaded with the equipment they'd "stolen" from Osborne, his dream was closer to reality than it had been less than 24 hours earlier. He had only victory and vengeance in mind. The Osbornes and Chumachenko focused on profits.

The Russians would pay large sums to equip their ghost armies. Elements in Ukraine would pay large sums to equip the militias. The Ukrainian government, on the sly, would pay large sums to arm the regular army. Everybody would get what they wanted, but the money didn't concern Draco.

But there was Aaron to deal with. His lack of commitment put everything at risk. The only way to achieve victory going forward meant Aaron had to be dealt with, too. Before his sensitivities brought more difficulty, and exposure.

Draco watched the waves. He knew what he had to do. But he had to wait until they reached Kerch. Once the ship docked, and the arms reached the Ukrainian units they planned to arm, all bets were off. They'd blow up a section of the Crimean Bridge so precious to Moscow, and watch the war begin anew. Then the Russians would see Draco's fury as they'd never seen it before.

33

Orest Chumachenko stood at the wide window of his penthouse office and surveyed his domain.

He felt like he owned Kerch. The biggest city in Crimea boasted plenty of industry and tourist opportunities, mostly thanks to him. Chumachenko had earned his fortune catering to the holiday needs of his fellow Russians.

Now, he was expanding into Crimea with very ambitious plans. But it was hard to thrive with the Nationalists carrying out their acts of aggression. The people of Crimea had voted to join Russia. The crazy "Yooks", as he called Ukrainians, held to the opinion such a vote didn't matter, had in fact been fixed. Nonsense.

Chumachenko wasn't much taller than five-foot-five, but he carried plenty of weight. Not the fleshy kind, either. At 50, he was well-muscled and trim thanks to hard work and dedication to his daily gym visits. His power came from his wealth, his Kremlin connections (forged by his father, a loyal party member in the old days), and his forceful personality. Chumachenko did not believe in the word "No".

When friends said he was nuts to build resorts in Kerch

before the Kremlin fully resolved the Nationalist problem, he said, "You're wrong." Chumachenko had a vision of Kerch becoming a greater tourist destination than any other. His vision began with a twin-tower resort on the coast of the Azov Sea where so many loyal comrades spent their holidays over the years.

The hot summers all but guaranteed visitors from the Motherland. They would want to experience all Kerch had to offer. He wouldn't only need to depend on the oligarchs for his income. But, yes, it would be ideal if Crimea was free of the "Yooks" who sought only to spoil and destroy.

For such a "cleansing of Crimea" he'd hatched, with his allies, another vision sure to bring about his primary goal.

Enter Father and Son Osborne.

But Osborne the Younger had left him very disappointed.

Chumachenko watched the city from his window. He could not see the construction near the Azov; what he saw instead was a city full of activity and bright lights. Yes, there were troops at almost every intersection. The population did not mind. The mostly Russian citizenry and loyal Ukrainians wanted no part of Nationalist nonsense. They looked at the soldiers and their vehicles and tanks as protection.

He wasn't worried about a war harming Kerch in general or Crimea in particular. Once the Crimean Bridge crumbled, the Russian Army would secure the peninsula. A blockage of Russian Navy ships would cut off all aid to Ukraine.

The Russian military would then bring retaliation to the Ukraine mainland. Kerch would see very little trouble as the Nationalists would run to join the fight over the border.

A blockade of Ukraine meant the government would need other sources of arms and supplies. Chumachenko and Osborne, and their proxies, would be there to save the day.

And Russia, with its continued reliance on mercenaries

and contract soldiers in the region, would spend money to equip those units too.

Chumachenko couldn't lose.

Somebody knocked on the door.

"Da," he called out.

He turned as the door opened and Vikka Malina entered.

The 46-year-old divorced mother of two had recently hitched her wagon to Chumachenko. They'd met at the gym. She might have been nearing 50 and produced two children, but she had the shape of a fit 20-year-old.

Vikka (short for Victoria) held a tablet computer. She said, "I have a report about the American."

"Bring it to my desk, my dear." He crossed ahead of her to where his large desk sat. He eased into his chair while Vikka took the one beside the desk and crossed her legs. She handed him the tablet.

Chumachenko donned a pair of reading glasses and read the screen. He scrolled with his thumb to advance each page.

"Dreadful," he said.

"Does this mean—"

He held up a hand and she paused her question. He finished reading, set the tablet on the desk, and removed his glasses. He stared ahead and said nothing for a long time, but his thoughts weren't as jumbled as one might expect. He knew what he had to do to preserve the plan.

The American, as Vikka called him, was Mark Osborne.

The report detailed his meetings with the FBI. The report did not indicate if the FBI suspected his role in the robbery. He had retained a lawyer, but was so far cooperating and answering questions.

They had planned for this to a certain point, but they were quickly traveling beyond the expected boundary into uncharted territory. The problems created by Aaron made Chumachenko doubt the original plan could work without adjustments. He'd wanted to use outsiders as a way to shield him from connection to the plot. At the rate events were going, if Mark Osborne found himself in a tight spot, exposure was certain.

"Orest?"

He turned to her. He smiled again. She made him happy. Vikka filled a void in his life, one caused by his dedication to work. He was lonely. Or had been, until he met Vikka. He had no children from prior relationships; had never married. At his age, he figured he would never accomplish either. But Vikka had two beautiful daughters. While they had their father in their lives, he took great joy in sharing his good fortune with them.

"You were going to ask me a question, my dear?"

"Does this report mean your plan is in jeopardy?"

She knew everything. He'd hidden nothing from her. She wanted the Nationalists out, too. They posed a danger to her kids.

He shook his head. "No."

"Are you certain?"

"I am certain."

"I believe you."

"Good. Won't be long now."

He rose. She followed him to the door. He promised to be home after he made an important call. He kissed her on the cheek and gave her rear end a pat as she left.

Chumachenko returned to his desk with his jaw clenched. He didn't like lying to Vikka, so he had to make sure the plan continued. Despite the hiccup. He picked up the phone and dialed a number from memory. A male voice answered.

"Yes?"

"It's me."

"Yes, sir. What do you require?"

"We have a problem in the United States and I'd like your best man to resolve the issue."

"I'm listening."

The conversation took ten minutes, and Chumachenko set in motion the solution to the problem.

Unfortunately, he could not reach Draco on the freighter. His other problem would have to wait.

34

US Secretary of State Peter Berry sat at his desk facing two large screen monitors.

One of his assistants fussed with connecting wires and cables. Berry paid him no mind as he thought about what he'd say to the Ukraine and Russian representatives. The president's order had been clear. Obtain cooperation to deal with the "Osborne threat". Berry hoped his experience would help him achieve the goal.

Nearing 68, Berry had built his reputation as a negotiator over his 40 years in the Senate. He was well-respected in DC circles, and now, as secretary of state, around the globe.

But none of it went to his head. Even the best had bad days. He needed to make sure this wasn't one of them. It would be much better if the Ukrainians and Russians solved the problem. If they refused to work together, he knew the CIA assets on the way had a better than even chance. He'd rather keep Americans out, but to prevent a war he understood the necessity of getting involved.

His assistant gave him a thumbs up, then established the

connections. Two men appeared on screens. Berry flashed his trademark smile.

"Good morning, gentlemen."

The two men on the monitors mumbled greetings. Then Vashkov, the Russian, took the meeting immediately off the rails.

"What is the meaning of this call, Mr. Secretary? I trust the United States isn't going to waste time telling us how wrong we are."

"Mr. Vashkov, the three of us have a mutual interest in the case of Mr. Osborne. I'm sure you've been informed?"

"We know of this latest Ukrainian trick, yes."

The Ukrainian representative muted the anger flashing across his face. But it came through in his words.

"This is not a trick! Ukraine has no knowledge of his plot, and we do not want any further bloodshed."

"You can't afford it," the Russian snapped.

Before he had a major argument on his hands, Berry appealed for calm.

"Please, gentlemen, a fight gets us nowhere. The US only learned of this situation 24 hours ago. What I'm hoping we can agree to is a joint task force effort to prevent a tragedy."

"Ukraine pledges all resources necessary to resolve the situation," the Ukrainian, Kolbochev, said.

"Russia will not agree to this," Vashkov replied. "I speak for my superiors when I tell you we will answer any act of aggression from Ukraine against Russian interests or its citizens with immediate retaliation. Up to *and including* full-scale invasion."

"Outrageous!" Kolbochev shouted. "We are not responsible for this problem. You know very well my government has ruled out military force at this time."

"*At this time*, Mr. Kolbochev. The Kremlin is well aware you are turning a blind eye to Nationalist forces in Crimea.

Until you disavow all hostile activity, a joint arrangement is out of the question."

Berry sighed. So much for respect and experience. He said, "Mr. Vashkov, I can assure you—"

"Empty words, Mr. Secretary! Your nation's sanctions on my country have caused irreparable harm to our economy. We are not interested in your assurances."

"The US cannot do this alone."

"The great American heroes have never hesitated to gallop in to save the day. Why hesitate now? We do not need you, Mr. Secretary. Russia will handle this problem. Good day."

The Russian blinked out.

"Mr. Secretary."

"Yes, Mr. Kolbochev."

"Crimea is a sensitive—"

"I'm aware your hands are tied. We won't hold it against you."

"Good luck, Mr. Secretary."

Berry signaled for his assistant to end the call. He folded his hands in front of his face. He'd never had a chance. The conflict was too intense to get either side to think clearly.

He'd have to report to the president that some days the dragon wins.

It was up to the CIA now, and Berry hoped they moved fast enough to prevent a world tragedy.

RAVEN AND TRACY listened to Clark Wilson's update during their layover at JFK. Raven wasn't surprised by the result of Berry's meeting. He wasn't surprised the Russians didn't want their help. The cover identities they traveled under would now be critical for staying off the radar. Wilson did have some good news. The CIA had managed to ping Aaron Osborne's cell phone. He was in Kerch on the waterfront, and Wilson promised to text the location to Raven's phone.

Wilson's update was top of mind when they touched down in Kerch at for-sale-and-currently-bankrupt-but-still-functioning airport named after the city it served. Raven and Tracy cleared customs and headed for baggage claim. They paused midstep as two people approached them at the carousel. They showed Russia federal identification. The man and woman claimed to be from the FSB, the internal security agency of the Russian Federation.

"I am Nadiya," said the woman, "and this is my partner Petro. We're here to take you to your hotel and coordinate your search effort."

Raven started to object; Tracy stopped him. "Much appreciated," she said. "Lead the way."

The two "Russians" walked ahead of them. Raven glared at Tracy. She mouthed, "What of it?"

He wanted to tell her everything wrong with following the pair. The Russians were a stubborn lot; no way they had changed their minds in such a short amount of time. This was a trap. They were compromised before stepping off the plane.

Which of course made perfect sense since the enemy knew they were coming. But Raven had at least wanted a chance to slip through the initial defense screen.

He also understood Tracy's willingness to go forward. Why look for the enemy when he could march you straight into his lair?

Best to see how it played out. But be ready for sudden and violent action, Raven decided.

The two agents helped them load their bags. Raven and Tracy sat in the back seat of the small sedan. No screen leapt from the floor to seal off the back while Petro switched on poison gas. The drive was actually uneventful with only light traffic. The terrain between the airport and city was undeveloped, and mostly untidy dirt lots dotted with unkempt greenery. Train tracks ran parallel to the road, and a cargo train kept pace with them for a while before disappearing into a tunnel. Raven noticed the huge presence of Russian troops once they entered city limits. The soldiers carried Kalashnikovs and appeared ready for action on every street. Some walked foot patrols. Others stood stationary. All were happily greeted by civilians going about their business.

At a stop light, Raven watched a young woman in an apron emerge from a coffee shop. She brought steaming cups to four soldiers stationed outside the door. The troops accepted the gift with smiles.

"They don't act oppressed," Tracy said.

Their hosts remained quiet despite the remark. Either they had nothing to say, or they weren't Russians. No Ruskie Raven had ever encountered would miss an opportunity to brag about the Motherland's military prowess.

"Any trouble here lately?" Raven said.

"Army makes sure there is no trouble," said Petro, who rode in the passenger seat. He was a wiry mouse-looking man with a narrow face framed by black hair. His eyes weren't the shifty, beady type, but they appeared dull and lifeless. As if he had been born to take orders from somebody else.

And perhaps Nadiya qualified as his master. She was shorter than Petro but her striking features and bright smile made her seem larger. With her petite figure and ponytail, she looked as if she might belong to a softball club instead of the Russian FSB. Then Raven laughed. He'd forgotten for a moment who they really were.

"What have you learned about Osborne?" Raven asked. "Any sign of him?"

"As far as we can tell," Petro said, "he has not arrived. The man with him, Draco, is known to us as well. In fact, he's wanted for questioning regarding the murders of two army sergeants. He won't slip through our net."

"You're watching the airport and the docks—"

Nadiya jumped in with a fiery glance at Raven in the rearview mirror. "We are watching everything, Mr. Raven. We do not need an American to tell us how to do our jobs."

"Hey. I'm only asking. We're on the same side, aren't we?"

"Of course," the woman said.

"Then you shouldn't mind me asking, Nadiya."

"While you are here, you will not do anything without first informing us. Do you understand me?"

"You're speaking English so I understand you perfectly."

"I am not in the mood for your jokes, Mr. Raven."

"And Tracy and I are not in the mood to be hamstrung. If Russia isn't taking this issue seriously, take us back to the airport and we'll leave on the next flight."

"No," Petro chimed. "We have our orders to help. Please understand the situation. It is very stressful here."

"I can tell."

Tracy said, "How much further to the hotel? I don't know about you all, but I sure need a drink."

"A fine idea," Raven echoed. "Let's have Uncle Sam buy the round. I'd hate to think we started on the wrong foot, right?"

"Yes," Nadiya agreed. "We will drink and settle down. There is much to do and we don't know how much time we have."

Raven glanced at Tracy. She was already looking at him. He winked.

35

AT THE HOTEL, PETRO ACCOMPANIED RAVEN TO HIS ROOM. Nadiya went with Tracy. Neither wanted them out of their sight, which was obvious to Raven as he set his suitcase on the bed. He didn't unlock the X-ray proof bottom of his suitcase where his replacement pistol resided. Better to not let the opposition see too much.

Raven announced he liked the room and they left. Tracy had the bug scanner. He was eager to see what the other side planted while they were out.

Raven and Petro stepped into the elevator for the ride to the lobby. There was a bar and lounge there. Raven had insisted they visit it instead of leaving the hotel.

"Did you grow up in Moscow?" Raven asked.

"Yes."

"I like Moscow. My favorite restaurant is right on the river. The Copperhead. Best steak in the world."

"Yes, it is very good. My father likes us to take him there for his birthday every year."

"How nice." Raven grinned. Petro didn't look at him. He watched the numbers above the door tick down to the lobby.

The women were already seated when Raven and Petro arrived. They sat on a small couch along a wall facing two plush chairs. A box-shaped table sat between them. Raven and Petro took the chairs. Tracy said she'd ordered everybody vodka on the rocks.

"Excellent," Raven said.

The bar wasn't full so they kept their voices low. The bar wanted to evoke a nightclub motif without the noise. The decorators had blacked out the walls, floor, and ceiling. Walkways outlined by strips of shrouded lights lined the floor. The parallel strips made the floor look like crisscrossing airport runways. *Is this a bar or the runway at LAX?* Raven thought.

"So your superiors told you what's going on," Raven said to their escorts, "and you know who our suspects are. Where do we find the big man, Chumachenko?"

"Try the phone directory," Petro said. "He's not hard to find."

Raven smiled at Tracy. "Never would have thought of that. You?"

"It might have shortened the hunt for bin Laden if only we'd looked in the phone book," she said.

Raven faced their escorts. "You'd think a fellow planning a catastrophe might hide in a volcano or something."

"No volcanoes here," Nadiya said.

"Good to know."

Raven watched the pair. Their faces remained stoic, not one hint of a smile. Language barrier? They spoke good English but didn't detect the sarcasm between Raven and Tracy. Typical Slavic Resting Bitch Face? Likely. Did they suspect they were being toyed with? Absolutely. They weren't trained operatives. They were point and shoot gophers. Petro had proved so in the elevator. Raven couldn't wait to tell Tracy how Petro miffed a simple trick.

Their escorts didn't stay for a second round and the invisible tension between the four did not loosen. All Raven knew was the opposition had them close; he supposed the opposite was true, as well. He and Tracy had to work the odds in their favor before the enemy closed the trap.

RAVEN UNLOCKED the bottom of his suitcase once he'd returned to the alleged safety of his hotel room. He removed the autoloader and shoulder harness provided by Clark. The gun was a Browning Hi-Power with several spare 13-round magazines. A box of nine-millimeter ammo accompanied the kit. Raven would have preferred a .45 pistol. But Clark knew Raven appreciated hand-crafted precision handguns; the Hi-Power qualified. He set the gun, ammo and harness in the nightstand drawer.

Tracy knocked on the door using a coded tap. He let her in. She had her right index finger in front of her mouth and the bug detector in her left hand. The small RF signal sweeper wouldn't only pick up bugs. If the enemy had planted small cameras, the RF sweeper would find them too. Tracy moved around the room with the device. A red light flashed. Devices present. Raven and Tracy went to each spot in the room where detection had occurred. They found no cameras. Bugs were in the nightstand phone, behind the dresser, and under the wall-facing desk.

Raven motioned for Tracy to follow him into the bath-room. He turned on the shower. As the noise of the rushing water filled the small space, he felt free to finally talk.

"Do you think we overdid it?"

"Oh, they know we're onto them," she said.

"Your phone bit was funny."

"I'm going to tell Clark we should try it some time."

"Petro blew it with me on the way down. I mentioned a restaurant in Moscow. It doesn't exist. He played along and said his father liked eating there."

"We're dealing with rookies!" she said. "Who falls for that old trick?"

"They're only meant to watch us. The other side thinks they have us in a box."

"Do they?"

"No way," Raven said. "But we need to hustle. Let's give it a few hours, and then I want to check out the address Clark sent. Follow behind me because I'm sure Nadiya and Petro aren't the only ones assigned to watch us."

"When do you think they'll make a move?" Tracy said.

"When they can control the hit," Raven said. "Too risky with all the army guys around. They'll take us somewhere saying they found a lead, and leave us there."

"Not if we shoot first."

"This will be fun."

"Not the word I'd use, Raven. But I know what you mean."

TRACY LEFT and Raven locked the door behind her. He'd left the shower running, and turned the water from cold to hot.

After relaxing under the spray, he stretched out on the bed. No sense calling Clark. The bugs would hear everything he said. Raven texted him instead with the update.

Clark: Can confirm no change from Moscow. Proceed with caution.

Raven: Duh.

Clark: I trust you'll work this situation in your favor.

Raven: Have I ever let you down? Wait, don't answer.
Clark: Ha.

Switching off the light, Raven went to sleep. He wanted a few hours of rest before checking the waterfront where the CIA had picked up Aaron's cell phone.

36

RAVEN LEFT THE KERCH HOTEL AFTER ONE A.M. THERE WAS still street traffic, but not much. As he stood in the front courtyard, the icy wind off the Kerch straight sliced through his jacket. He watched the winking port lights in the distance. The cranes were well lit; between the hotel and the port was Detskiy Park. The park's trees blocked most of the port, but not the cranes scratching against the black sky.

The cranes weren't the only sights against the black. Raven looked to the right. The twin arches of the Crimean Bridge were lit in bright white light. He pressed his lips together. The bridge so reviled by Ukraine while cheered by Moscow. The presumed target of Aaron Osborne and Yakiv Draco.

The span connected Russia to Crimea, solidifying the Motherland's hold on the peninsula. It was a source of pride for the Russians and a thorn in the side for Ukraine.

Construction began in 2014 with completion in 2018. The bridge reduced travel time between the two nations to fifteen minutes. You could drive or take a train. Russia loved it. Ukraine had claimed, even as construction took place, the bridge would never be completed, and was nothing more than Ruskie propaganda. When the first cars from the Russian side made the crossing, Russian media mocked Ukraine for doubting the determination of the Kremlin.

Blowing up a portion of either side of the span would make Russia's blood boil. The business of war demanded one know how to manipulate opposing sides into going full speed ahead with an already simmering conflict. Raven figured Osborne, Draco, and Chumachenko had calculated such manipulation to an expert level.

He had to stop them.

Commotion caught Raven's attention. Voices, laughter. He crossed the courtyard to the sidewalk and followed the sounds. Next door to the hotel was a nightclub. "Cherri" the sign said. A cluster of young men and women outside suggested the inside was too full, so they partied outside. None of them were dressed for the sharp breeze; none seemed to notice. Raven figured he was too old to be immune to cold any longer. Or maybe they were used to it. They lived in Kerch, after all. Two taxi cabs made U-turns down the street and pulled up at the club. Three young women climbed into one while the other deposited a lone man who greeted pals waiting for him.

Nightlife wasn't huge in Kerch. Most of the city's sites were best seen during the day. Nature areas, the wide land-scape beyond the city, and the coast. Most of the city turned in after nine at night. But it was nice to see some activity. Raven didn't feel alone.

He had no car. He planned to catch one of the late buses. He carried no gun. He didn't want any potential entangle-ment with the Russian army. And if they found him with a firearm, there'd be trouble no cover ID could explain. He carried his passport, visa, and ID. If need be, he was an American tourist taking a walk because of jet lag.

Such a strategy presented other problems, but Raven wasn't sure he'd face such issues yet. Time to find out. Worst case, he'd take a gun off any member of the opposition who felt like taking a shot at him.

He glanced around the courtyard behind him. The light of the hotel's sign gave the space an orange glow. Right away he spotted two others hanging around. Trees concealed them, but they were no doubt waiting for him. Watchers left behind by Nadiya and mousy Petro. Time for a little fun.

At a break in traffic, Raven jogged across Kirova Street and hopped over the low wall of Detskiy Park. A children's playground greeted him. Off to the left, a grassy area; plenty of trees filled the landscape. There were a lot of trees in Kerch, Raven noticed. The city builders had not chopped down every single one in the establishment of the city. It presented the idea of urban and nature co-existing. New York City might learn a thing or two from the idea. Of course, they wouldn't. Chop it all down! Bye, bitches! Steel, glass, and concrete forever!

Streetlamps on the sidewalk lit the way as he cut left toward the grass. Part of the interior had little illumination, but some light from the port spilled over. The low light created moving shadows as trees rustled in the breeze from the strait.

Raven jogged across soft grass and stopped behind a tree trunk. He looked back. The two men from the courtyard were sprinting across the street. They ran through the playground, then turned in Raven's direction. Their hands were still empty. Raven waited. Behind him, the dark ended at another street; beyond the pavement, the port. He could lose the pair, or deal with them. A fight was not what he wanted. Yet.

Raven left the tree and continued. His shoes scraped on a concrete path dividing the grass, and he rolled to a bush. He scanned the semi-darkness but no moving outlines announced themselves. Then a man began speaking, fast, acknowledging a radio call. The pair were part of a larger team. Great. He'd told Tracy to wait a half hour before leaving so he could get the watchers away from the building. Now he knew there were others waiting for her too. She'd have to be on her toes. Raven didn't dare risk a text message to warn her. His phone screen would light up his position in the park.

But the pair still remained concealed, until one crossed into view. He was alone. They were splitting up. The man Raven watched approached the strip of concrete. He paused, taking a knee, and scanned the area. Raven wore dark clothes, and Watcher One had the port lights to mess with his vision. Raven might as well have been invisible. But his fortune would change as soon as Watcher One moved closer. He'd deal with Watcher Two later. While he had a chance to take one out of action, he decided to do so.

Watcher One rose and advanced in a path taking him wide of Raven's spot. Raven shifted as a blast of wind shook the trees. Watcher One stopped, turned Raven's way, and pulled something from under his jacket. The port lights glinted off the stainless-steel of the man's handgun. An extension on the barrel was a suppressor. They didn't have orders to take, or leave, Raven alive.

Raven waited and watched. The man approached the bush. Raven wondered if his legs created a different kind of shadow, one out of place with the rest. He couldn't hide forever. If he wanted a look at the spot where the CIA detected Aaron's cell phone, he had to get rough sooner rather than later.

Raven moved his left hand. He grabbed a handful of dirt

from under the bush. Pulling his hand back, he snapped a twig. Watcher One ran at him.

Raven jumped up and met the watcher midway. He threw the dirt. Watcher One dodged, but some of the dirt hit where intended, in the face. He let out a yell as flecks entered one of his eyes, and Raven closed a fist and swung.

37

Raven landed a solid punch between the flaps of the man's open jacket. He connected with Watcher One's gut. Air rushed out of the man as he swung his pistol at Raven's head. Raven ducked, grabbing the arm with both hands and twisting. He pulled the arm behind Watcher One's back. The man bent backward, yelling again. Not in pain, but for his partner. Raven reached for the gun, but then Watcher Two arrived. Watcher One kicked at Raven's right leg. Pulling the pistol free, Raven fired at Watcher Two.

The suppressed pistol shot sounded like a loud snap, and the bullet missed. Raven still achieved a desired result. Watcher Two dived for cover.

Raven pivoted and broke into a run for the port. Pistol snaps behind Raven signaled more shots. Raven weaved, reaching the pavement and racing across to the parking lot of a building. A line of trees covered the front of the building. Raven entered the shadows they offered, and moved along the wall to the corner. He ran again. A jetty lay ahead with boats docked on either side. At the end of a longer jetty adjacent sat a silent freighter. Raven kept moving. More lights meant he was easier to see. Less trees meant he was an easier target.

He reached a walkway with an iron railing to prevent falls into the water. More jetties, bigger boats, and tall cranes all around. He ran ahead. A darkened building twenty yards away looked good. He didn't look back. Stopping in an alcove, Raven held the pistol beside his leg and watched the way he'd come. It didn't take long for the watchers to appear, with Watcher One staying behind his armed partner.

Raven glanced at the pistol. It was a foreign make he didn't recognize, one more familiar to Eastern Europe. He hoped it proved reliable. The thick grip told him the magazine was of high capacity, but he didn't know how many rounds remained.

Raven looked around. Open space in front of him with an area of overgrowth. Off to the right, more of the port, but he'd be exposed as soon as he left the alcove. The only good news was the terrain didn't favor the watchers, either. He decided to make a stand where he was and get back to Kirova Street.

The watchers continued their approach. When they were finally within twenty yards, Raven made his move.

He raised the gun and fired once. Watcher Two shouted, and as Watcher One hit the ground, Two met Raven's challenge. Raven's shot had missed, and as he put pressure on the trigger once more, nothing happened. A glance at the gun explained the issue. The slide had not returned to battery. The gun had jammed while cycling a cartridge. Raven was holding a paperweight.

There was nowhere to run, so Raven charged. At the same time, he snapped back the slide to eject the jammed cartridge. Watcher Two fired hastily and the round whispered over Raven's head. By then he collided with Watcher Two and took him to the ground.

Watcher Two deflected Raven's blows and pushed his gun arm away. He smacked Raven on the side of the head with his own autoloader. Raven felt the blow. It stunned him, made his eyes spin, but Two hadn't delivered the strike with 100% force. Watcher Two still had a grip on Raven's right arm. The pistol might not be jammed any longer, but Raven couldn't get the weapon into action. Watcher Two pulled his right arm back and pointed his gun at Raven's face.

And then Watcher One joined the fight.

With a yell he charged Raven, tackling him, rolling across the ground with Raven underneath and then on top, then underneath again. The gun flew from Raven's hand. Watcher One struck Raven's face once before Raven returned the favor, hitting as hard as he could. Watcher One grabbed for Raven's head. Two gained his feet and yelled for his partner to get out of the way. Watcher One lifted Raven's head to bash it on the pavement. Raven slipped his hands between the man's arms and forced the grip apart. Raven slammed the heel of his palm into Watcher One's chin and the blow forced One back. He rolled away. Watcher Two lined Raven up in his sights.

Men started yelling. Watcher Two held up his hands and yelled something to Watcher One. A spotlight shined on them. More voices joined in, men shouting for Two to drop the gun. The voices were many, speaking with authority, and Raven turned his body to look. Four uniformed soldiers with Kalashnikovs ran at them. The one who held the light shouted louder than his comrades.

The soldiers circled them. The watchers raised their hands. Raven stayed on the ground as the soldiers told the two men to get on their knees. The watchers complied. The man with the spotlight shined the beam in Raven's face, and gave him the same orders.

"I'm unarmed," Raven told them. He sat up and held out his empty hands. "I'm an American tourist! Tourist!"

The soldier with the spotlight took out his pistol and told Raven not to move. Then he told another to use his radio and call their superior officer.

Raven began running his rap. The troops didn't understand a word but he needed to get his story going. While the soldier with the pistol covered Raven, the others questioned the watchers. Their words were harsh. They had the armed pair in a tight spot. Somebody found One's gun and held onto it.

Moments later, the commanding officer arrived in a UAZ-469 with the roof removed. He left the vehicle and approached the group. The man covering Raven spoke a few words, and the officer nodded. He told him to put his pistol away and addressed Raven.

"You're American?"

"Yes."

"What are you doing here?"

"Jet lag. Couldn't sleep. I walked to the park and these two came after me."

"You shouldn't be out after dark."

"No shit."

"Identification, please."

Raven didn't have to pretend to shake. The blow to the head made him unsteady. The officer helped him to his feet and let him lean against the hood of the UAZ. Raven produced his papers. The officer whistled for the man with the light, who came running to shine the light on Raven's papers.

"You are journalist?"

"Here on assignment, yeah."

"Hmmm."

"My papers are in order," Raven said.

The officer made no comment as he examined the items. He said something to the soldier with the light, who turned it off. The officer handed back Raven's stuff.

"It can be dangerous after dark," the officer said. "I'm sorry for your jet lag, but you should have stayed in your hotel."

Raven nodded.

"I will have one of my men look at the wound on your head. It's bleeding."

Raven felt the gash. His fingers came away wet with blood. "It's okay. I've suffered worse."

"You might have a concussion."

"I swear I'm fine. I'll go back to the hotel and sleep it off."

"Our apologies. We try to keep the streets clear of this." He gestured dismissively at the watchers. The pair now had their hands zip-tied behind their backs. Neither looked enthusiastic.

"Enjoy the rest of your stay in Kerch."

"I'll try."

"What is your assignment?"

Raven forced a laugh. "We're doing a special on the new tourist resorts you're building."

"I trust this unfortunate incident won't factor into your reporting."

"No. And I will tell my colleagues to stay indoors at night."

"We would appreciate it. Can you find your way back?"

"It's across the street. Hotel Kerch."

"Ah, yes, very nice there."

Raven stood back with the officer while his men loaded the watchers into the UAZ. The driver took them and some of the soldiers away. The officer snapped orders, and the rest followed on foot. With a final goodbye, the officer left Raven. He stood a moment to watch them go. He still felt unsteady, his vision tilting, but the sensation would pass.

He had no intention of going back to the hotel. He wasn't done for the night.

38

THE ADDRESS PROVIDED BY CLARK WILSON WAS A BUILDING AT Port Kavkas. It was a few miles from the hotel on Kirova Street, but not close enough to walk.

When Raven reached the street, the outdoor party at "Cherri" was still going. Music from inside filtered outside. Raven used a handkerchief to stop the blood from his wound. He'd cleaned away the worst using a water fountain in the park playground.

There was still the question of who the watchers had communicated with. The smart thing to do would be to follow the Russian officer's suggestion of going back to his room. Raven instead caught a bus. He sat on the left aisle to hide his head wound. Nobody on the bus noticed. The late workers were few, and most stared at their phone screens.

He wondered how Tracy was doing. She should have left by now.

He watched the passing port through the right-side windows. The tinted windows made it tough to pick out any specific exterior features. When the bus made its next stop, he hopped off. Alone. The bus rumbled away leaving only the breeze for company.

Raven started walking, checking addresses as he moved. After a block he found the building he was looking for. The front of the building was dark, but lights lit the rear. A chain-link fence blocked access to the back. Raven walked along the fence looking for anything unusual. He didn't expect to run into Aaron, but if he had been to the place, there had to be a reason why.

TRACY EXITED the hotel 20 minutes after Raven. She was too anxious to sit still. Also, unlike him, she carried her pistol. The gun rode in the harness under her jacket.

She'd called a taxi and met the driver outside. Giving him the Port Kavkaz address, she sat alert but relaxed.

The driver sped along Kirova Street at a fast clip. She only had a brief look at the activity outside Club Cherri and wished she had more time for a social life. But there were more important things to do than party; it was the reason she worked so much.

Tracy looked back through the rear window. Only a few cars, but any one of them might have been—

One *was* following. The driver of a black Audi weaved around cars until it was two car lengths behind the taxi. A chill of excitement raced up her neck. Raven might have drawn away some of the surveillance crew, but they had back-up. She sat forward and wondered how many were in the Audi.

Time to lay her pre-planned snow job on the driver.

"Hey, I'm at the hotel hiding from my husband. Can you make a few turns? I think he's behind us."

"We will lose him," the driver said with a grin. "I am best driver in Kerch, don't worry."

Tracy started to say thank you but before she had the words out the driver made a sharp left. He cut across the opposite lane to continue up a perpendicular street. The scenery flashed by, mostly dark apartment buildings.

"Yup, somebody is following us, miss."

Tracy turned in her seat. Another vehicle closed fast. She couldn't ID the car but the headlight pattern looked like the Audi's. There was no reason to doubt it was the Audi.

Another sharp turn. This time to the right, with tires screeching. Hard brake; the driver twisted the wheel left; the cab bumped the edge of the curb going into a narrow alley.

Only the cab's headlamps sliced a path through the dark alley. Tracy's breath quickened and she sank in the seat. The brick walls on either side seemed to close in; Tracy gasped. But then the wheels screeched onto asphalt again as the driver hooked right. He continued along a residential street lined with trees and parked cars.

"Check back, miss," the driver said. Tracy caught his reflection in the rearview mirror. He was grinning.

Tracy looked. Nothing behind them but dark street.

"Great," she said. "I owe you a big tip."

"No charge," the driver said. "That was fun!"

Tracy thought of the pistol under her jacket and how she might have needed it if the driver screwed up or if the enemy had been a little better.

You don't know what you missed, pal.

RAVEN SAW no sign the chain-link fence was electrified. He picked a spot forty yards away and climbed over. The barbed wire on top stabbed through his clothes but he ignored the discomfort. Landing on the other side, he wiped his hands on his jeans and headed for a building nearby.

A sign in Cyrillic hung in front advising the building was for lease. He watched the warehouse from the doorway, noting, for the first time, its high domed roof. Lights on inside. Most of the brightness was in the rear facing the water. At the jetty sat a large freighter with a ramp connecting to the jetty's plank. A crane extended from the port over the freighter's bow. Had Aaron and Draco brought the stolen explosives and weapons to Kerch using the ship? It made sense, though he wondered where they'd departed from since Nevada was landlocked.

The side of the warehouse he faced had a few doors at ground level. Two sets of stairs ended at doors on the second floor. He wanted to get closer, get inside.

He waited. Raven wondered where Tracy was. Then he stopped wondering, and stopped thinking, as a pair of sentries appeared. They came from the rear and stopped at each of the ground floor doors, tugging on doorknobs. Both men spoke quietly, but Raven only picked out a few words at his distance. The word which stood out the most was "inventory". And the crew wasn't happy about working late.

Both lit cigarettes and stood smoking and complaining and gossiping. Raven remained in the shadow of the empty building. Where was Tracy?

After a few minutes, the two sentries flicked away their smokes and headed back to the rear of the building. Raven gave them an extra minute and broke cover. He crossed the distance, taking cover again about ten yards from the side. A stack of pallets near the fence provided his shield this time. Another pause and scan.

Headlights flashed on the pallets before shifting away. A car stopped in front of the warehouse. A black Audi. Four men exited, and a fifth met them at the front door.

The fifth man said, "What happened?"

Raven stayed put. The driver gave the report. He explained the two "who went after Raven" didn't come back, and "the woman" hopped in a cab and they lost her.

The fifth man told the four to keep their weapons handy. Nobody inside was able to stop what they were doing to stand guard. The Americans might come snooping, the man continued. The Audi crew drew side arms and followed the fifth man inside.

Great.

Then again, Raven decided, the arrival of the gun crew presented an opportunity. For distraction. Their arrival might make the rest look the other way a moment and allow Raven a chance to slip through.

Raven left the pallets and hurried for a set of stairs.

39

RAVEN TOOK THE STEPS TWO AT A TIME. HE FELT THE STRAIN when he reached the top, but didn't slow down. Testing the doorknob, he felt it turn. He slipped inside. Nobody waited opposite. He pulled the door closed behind him.

He squatted on the metal walkway. Ahead off his left, an empty office with the lights on. Below, a different story.

Crates. A lot of crates. They bore Osborne Defense stencils on the sides. Most were open. On the warehouse floor lay the contents. A small number of men counted items, made notes on clipboards, and examined each piece of equipment.

Rifles and machine guns of various makes. A stack of C-4. The blocks of plastic explosive must have been two feet high. Cases of ammunition. Enough ordnance to equip a small battalion.

The gun crew from the Audi and the fifth man entered. The fifth man ordered them to spread out, check outside now and then, and stay out of the way.

Raven remained close to the wall and away from the edge

of the walkway. He didn't want to be seen if somebody looked up. What he wanted next was a peek in the office. The voices below echoed, the counting resuming with the arrival of the gun crew. Raven's pulse beat hard. With the gunners on scene, getting out might be tougher than getting inside. How long before the gunners checked the office and upstairs doors? Had Raven been down there, it would be first priority.

The office had two desks on either side of the doorway. They were desks made of steel, very heavy, the kind of industrial strength stuff not found in executive office suites. Raven checked papers, notes. He found a yellow customs form clearing the arrival of the creates. He doubted whoever signed off had done more than collect the bribe to apply his signature.

Leaning against the wall on the other side of the desk were a pair of AK-74U short-barreled rifles. Raven picked one up. He checked the chamber. A cartridge sat at the ready. Might come in handy.

Raven moved to the second desk. More papers.

Somebody yelled.

Raven dropped beside the desk. He set his finger on the 74U's trigger. Somebody found the unlocked second-level door. Footsteps pounded the walkway, growing in volume. Heading for the office. The gunner stepped through the doorway. He turned his head to the right and froze when he saw Raven.

But he didn't freeze for long. When he brought up his pistol, Raven fired over the top of the desk. The 74U flashed a tongue of flame and knocked the gunner back against the opposite desk. He tumbled to the floor.

Shouting below. Raven jumped over the body and ran to the walkway. He fired a second burst over the rail. The men below scattered, yelling all at once. Raven ran. Pistol shots cracked, smacking the wall beside Raven as he ran. He fired a third burst and the 74U clicked empty. He dropped the weapon and ran hard for the door from which he'd entered.

Crashing through, Raven leaned against the rail and slid toward the ground—much faster than he'd thought. As his feet hit the pavement, one of the doors ahead began to open. Raven turned and slipped under the stairs. Two gunners exited, pistols in hand, their heads turning left and right. They split up. One came toward the stairs. Raven met him and swung a fist into the side of his head. He caught the man as he fell, grabbing his pistol. He hoped this gun worked. The second gunman turned his way. Raven fired. The second man sprouted a third eye between the two he'd been born with.

Raven sprinted for the empty building next door which now seemed like a million miles away. More gunfire snapped behind him as the last of the four gunners exited the rear.

Raven tripped on a crack in the pavement and crashed, the pistol flying from his hand. Winded, he didn't stop moving. He rolled left, scrambled to his feet, and cursed. Another figure appeared ahead and raised a gun. Raven blinked as the new arrival fired twice. None of the shots hit him. But they did hit the gunman. The shooter smacked the pavement face first.

"Come on, Raven!"

Tracy!

He ran to her.

"What kept you?"

"Is that a thank you I heard?"

"Thanks, but let's get out of here."

They ran.

BACK AT RAVEN'S hotel room, they found each bug and crushed them into the carpet. Tracy dropped into a chair while Raven paced. He told her of his discovery and then the story of Watchers One and Two. She told him about her taxi ride.

"You need to be more careful," she said. "You keep charging like a bull into places and almost getting killed. If I hadn't shown up, you'd be dead."

"Nuts, I've had all the fun. Did you get a date with the cab driver?"

"Shut up."

"At least we know the weapons are here. If they plan to blow up the bridge, they have plenty of access from the port."

"If they don't clear out."

"They won't. They'll try for us again. All cards are on the table now. Nobody's fooling anybody any longer."

"Will you settle down already?"

He sighed and sat across from her. There was a small table between them. "I could use a drink."

"Little late for that."

"Or early. Back home it's daytime."

She laughed. "And not even five o'clock yet."

"We both need some sleep. Keep your weapon handy."

"Where was yours tonight?"

"Here in the room, and if the Russians had caught me carrying, I'd be in the same cell with the other two clowns."

Tracy left the chair and started for the door. "Try not to get killed again, Raven."

"Hey."

She turned.

"Will you call me Sam already?"

"Make me."

She went out. Raven laughed and locked the door. He

turned in and fell to sleep without delay. Action was the best jet lag cure ever.

40

RAVEN AND TRACY SAT IN THE HOTEL COFFEE SHOP OVER
breakfast. Both looked exhausted. When Nadiya and Petro
joined them, they hoped their state wasn't too obvious.
Nadiya fought hard to hide a grin. Raven knew she knew.

"Late night?" Nadiya said.

Tracy looked to Raven. Raven gave her the same excuse
he'd used overnight. "Jet lag."

"Oh, yes, horrible thing."

"Did you two get breakfast?"

She said they did but could use more coffee. Raven waved
over their waitress who took the order and departed.

"Are you sure it's only jet lag making you tired?" Nadiya
said. Her partner Petro sat without speaking, and Raven
didn't like how he examined their faces. They were the ones
playing games now, but Raven saw how he and Tracy could
throw it right back at them.

"Well, we were a little busy last night, right, honey?"

Tracy blanched.

"We can tell them, don't you think?"

"You ass."

"Well—"

Tracy cut him off. "It's supposed to be a *secret*, dammit."

"Why keep secrets from our new friends?" Raven smiled. To Nadiya, "Right? We should all four be honest with each other."

"We won't tell," Nadiya said. "Even Petro has a lover in the service, don't you?"

"Nobody cares," Petro finally said. The waitress brought their coffee.

"What's the plan for today?" Raven said to change the subject.

"We know where Osborne is hiding," Nadiya told them. "Why don't we go take a look?"

"Where are we going?" Raven remained cool but he saw Tracy tense. Worse, Petro saw her too.

"Warehouse at Port Kavkaz," Nadiya said. "Our informants tell us a freighter docked there a little over 24 hours ago. Customs may have been bribed to look the other way."

Raven laughed. Tracy's eyes widened.

"This we have to see," Raven said. "Finish your coffee and we'll go. Which one of you is driving?"

Petro said he'd drive.

This time, Raven had the Hi-Power on him.

The warehouse looked different in the daylight. Raven hadn't noticed its battleship gray paint in the middle of the night.

They parked across the street, watching people arrive and leave, but there was no sign of Aaron or Draco.

What they did see was frustrating. The game continued. Nadiya and Petro must have been laughing themselves silly on the inside.

Somebody opened the gate in the fence. Raven and Tracy watched two pairs of trucks, with covered beds, leave the property. Raven took a deep breath to settle his rising anger. They were moving the weapons and explosives, distributing to cells in the field. And they were doing it under the noses of him and Tracy. There was nothing they could do. The little overnight soft probe had been for naught. All they'd done was make the enemy move up their transport time. Nadiya and Petro were there to throw it in their faces.

"I don't suppose your informant mentioned they were moving stuff today?" Raven asked. He and Tracy sat in the back seat.

"No," Petro said from behind the wheel.

"Any idea where the stuff is going? Could be important."

"We will check," Nadiya said. She told Petro to hit the road.

They got stuck in a traffic jam on the way back to the hotel. Russian military vehicles lined the side of the road. They were checking cars, hauling out passengers, and throwing them against the military trucks. Each person was frisked. Others were questioned off to the side. Other soldiers waved cars through. They weren't stopping all.

"City-wide sweep," Nadiya reported. "The Russian navy has sent more ships into the strait as well, to protect the bridge. No boats will get near the span."

Which is why they needed to clean out the warehouse, Raven thought. If they couldn't use a boat to send out a crew to plant bombs on the Crimean Bridge, what other means might they have?

Or was he wrong and the bridge wasn't the target, but instead a decoy?

"When can we see Chumachenko?" Tracy asked once they'd passed through the delay.

"Tonight," Nadiya said. "We know where he'll be having dinner. His wife and associates will be there too."

"Can't wait," Raven said.

DRACO DROVE while Aaron Osborne sat in the passenger seat. The truck traveled north heading out of the city. The back of the truck held automatic weapons for a Ukrainian civilian militia. Some of Draco's old comrades in arms made up the group leadership. The goal was to have the militia resupplied before they blew up the Crimean Bridge. And re-sparked the conflict.

Aaron sat with his window open and made no attempt to talk to Draco. The Ukrainian merc had not said much since breakfast, when Chumachenko called. The big boss did not ask to speak with Aaron but only to Draco. The big boss was furious about the security breach at the warehouse. Aaron knew it had happened because they were stringing along Raven and Tracy. Aaron didn't understand why they were waiting to get rid of them. The Russian occupiers made the situation difficult, sure. They had to make decisions carefully, and plan action to the last detail. Confrontation with the Russians was a no-no. Until it didn't matter any longer. But Aaron feared they were waiting too long.

Aaron was aware of another possibility. He might not return from this trip, and he sweated thinking of a way out. With Draco's militia pals, he'd be one against…too many to have a chance. Aaron only knew what Draco had told him. If Chumachenko gave him other instructions, they weren't spoken.

Draco picked up the highway out of Kerch. The city faded behind them. Rolling hills full of green took its place.

Aaron told himself to calm down. If they wanted to be rid of him, they'd have done it already. Whacking one of their own wasn't as tough as Raven and Tracy.

Aaron began to sweat a little more. No amount of thinking reassured him.

Draco stopped. They were on a dirt road with wilderness all around. Soldiers with rifles wearing gray camo stepped into the path. Draco threw the truck into park. "Get out," he said.

Aaron's heart skipped. The edge in Draco's voice made him wonder if he'd be left here. Draco might hand him over to the militia and tell them to get rid of him...

Stop it.

Draco hopped out. Aaron saw in the side mirror the others as they left their trucks. He exited too. The cold air dried the sweat on his face and neck. He wondered how the back of his shirt looked.

41

DRACO APPROACHED THE GROUP. HE SHOOK HANDS WITH THE leader and they spoke warmly in rapid Ukrainian. Aaron and the other four from the convoy stood off the road. Draco and the leader continued their conversation. The militiamen cast nervous glances at Aaron and the others. Aaron kept his hands free and in the open. He wanted to avoid the reaction of a jumpy soldier with his finger on the trigger of a rifle.

Aaron decided the militia crew wasn't in terrible shape. Their uniforms were clean, not shabby as he'd have expected. They were not professional soldiers, but they took their role seriously. No missing buttons or untucked cuffs. Most importantly, their rifles were clean and not showing signs of neglect or abuse.

Draco and the team leader concluded their chat. Draco returned to the trucks as the militia started up the road at a quick pace.

"We'll follow them," Draco said, "and transfer the weapons to their vehicles."

Back in the trucks. Slow drive along the rough road.

Aaron had noticed a lot of young faces in the group. Most

had been older. The young ones were eager to defend their land from invasion. Well, he'd help give them the opportunity to achieve glory.

Assuming he lived long enough.

The convoy reached a clearing in the forest. Two large half-tracks waited. The convoy crew sat as the militia transferred weapons, ammunition, and explosives. They didn't have all the C-4, of course. Most of the plastic explosive had been taken elsewhere.

It was on the drive back to Kerch when Draco finally spoke.

"You're on thin ice."

"I figured," Aaron said.

"Chumachenko has a plan to take care of our problems. It starts tonight."

"Good."

"Everything will be settled tonight."

Aaron wasn't sure how to respond. But he decided he should prepare for any outcome.

He still had Raven's gun.

———

DRACO'S REMARK ABOUT "TONIGHT" was relative. It was ten o'clock in the morning in Sparks. A few minutes after ten, the assassin hired by Chumachenko murdered Mark and Brenda Osborne.

Osborne the Elder handed his wife the breakfast dishes and finished clearing the table. She loaded the dishwasher.

"I'll be late," he said. "I have a video conference tonight and they will go long, I'm sure."

"Don't you have another meeting with your lawyer, too?"

"Tomorrow at three."

"Oh, okay."

The doorbell rang. Worry flashed over Brenda's face.

Osborne shook his head. "I sure hope the FBI isn't here." Brenda offered a weak smile. Osborne left the kitchen.

The days since the "robbery" had been tough. Osborne figured he was always one misstep away from getting arrested.

Morale at the company was low, too. The Feds were questioning everybody, looking for anyone guilty, and Osborne had to keep quiet and watch. He tried to reassure his people via memo and pep talks. But he saw too much doubt in their eyes. His people were worried about their jobs and paychecks and families, and he couldn't blame them.

Chumachenko had warned this might happen, they'd worked out a response, and they'd be all right if they stuck to the plan.

Osborne took a deep breath to steady himself as he approached the door. Stand tall. Be proud. Look 'em in the eye and lie. They were looking for Aaron, he knew, and might have found him. He'd deal with the consequences if it turned out to be true, and get his son the best legal help. Or he'd help Aaron vanish.

He opened the door expecting two federal agents.

Only one man stood on the porch, a swarthy fellow in a long black coat inappropriate for the warmth of the morning.

"Who are—"

The man jerked a suppressed pistol from his right coat pocket and shot Osborne once. The bullet caved in Osborne's face and pushed it out of the back of his head. His body hit the floor with a loud thud.

The assassin stepped over the body and avoided the mess as he advanced into the house.

"Mark?"

The woman stepped into the hallway and screamed. The assassin raised his gun. He fired once and her scream ended.

The assassin departed without closing the front door. He drove away and took the highway further into the mountains where he stopped long enough to dig a hole. He buried his shoes and coat. There were spares in the car. He continued driving and didn't return to Sparks.

TRACY LAUGHED. "GIN!" She slapped the cards on the table.

Raven shook his head. "That's three times you've beaten me. I'm impressed." He gathered the cards to shuffle.

"I used to play—"

She stopped.

"Hmmm?"

"Never mind."

"Please, tell me." Raven ruffled the cards on the tables.

"I used to play with my father all the time."

"Beat him a lot?"

"Not when I was a kid, but when I got older, I gave him a run for his money. We moved around a lot—he was in the army. He taught me gin to help make the moves a little easier, you know?"

"I do indeed. Spent plenty of time on army bases growing up, remember?"

"Yes, you mentioned it."

"We haven't exactly spent much time getting to know one another, Tracy."

"It's hard for me."

"I understand. Where is your father now? Retired?"

"Missing."

Raven raised an eyebrow.

She dropped her eyes to the table. "He was in Afghanistan

with his unit. There was a fight, and they never found him after. I don't know if he's alive or dead."

"I'm so sorry."

"It's why I've stayed with intelligence work," she said. "I'm trying to find out what happened."

"Thank you for telling me. When this is over—"

"What?" She looked up. "You'll wave a magic wand?"

"Tracy—"

"What can you do that I haven't done in the last ten years?"

"Two heads are better than one. A new perspective might help. If there's a clue you missed, I can catch the detail."

"Deal the cards, Raven. We have another half hour before dinner."

"At least think it over. I'm sure I can help."

"Maybe."

"Sounds like you've given up."

"No," she said, "but there hasn't been much to encourage me to keep going lately."

Raven shuffled and let the conversation fade. If she wanted help she'd ask. He couldn't force her to accept his offer.

She said, "Do you have a plan for tonight?"

"Oh, yes." Raven began dealing. "I'm going to shake their cages and get the fireworks going."

"I like fireworks."

"We're running out of time. If they moved the ordnance, you know it's been delivered to whoever is carrying out the attack."

"Not Aaron and Draco?"

"I expect they will be far from whatever happens."

They looked at their cards but didn't make any moves. Tracy set her cards down.

"All I want is my father back, Raven."

"Uh-huh."

"It's why I don't connect with other people. Once you lose somebody—"

"I know."

"Do you?"

Raven felt the weight of the locket around his neck. He made no move to show her, though. "More than you think," he said.

They played, but Raven's mind wasn't on the game. The life they led might have its rewards, but pain was a trade-off too.

Raven's phone rang. Nadiya said she and Petro were waiting for them in the lobby.

42

DINNER WAS AT A FANCY PLACE RAVEN COULDN'T PRONOUNCE and didn't care to try. All he knew was Orest Chumachenko was a few tables away. He had a plan to upset the big shot's night.

Nadiya and Petro made small talk while they waited for drinks. Raven let Tracy give the non-committal responses. Chumachenko and his entourage were having a grand old time at their table. Their jovial exclamations combined with the noise in the crowded restaurant. The wait staff didn't take the loud volume well. They wore expressions of resignation at the audible assault their eardrums suffered. Raven noticed one busboy wearing earplugs.

Finally, Petro, who sat nearest to Raven, leaned close and pointed out the players.

"Chumachenko is at the head of the table," the mousy man said. "On his right is his wife, Vikka. She has two daughters Chumachenko dotes on, much to the annoyance of their father."

"Why?"

"He can't afford the same gifts Chumachenko provides. He's afraid they will think he's not good enough."

"Some fathers worry too much," Raven said. "His kids won't do that."

"The rest are Chumachenko's business associates. His accountant, his lawyer. Nobody we suspect of being involved with planning the attack."

"Sure."

"Your two friends aren't there."

"So?" Raven said. He hadn't expected to see Aaron or Draco and wasn't disappointed. "I'm sure they won't be hard to find once we take care of the boss."

Tracy watched while half-listening to Nadiya. Tracy was waiting for him to act. He'd told her to be ready to improvise.

He was waiting for the right opportunity, a seat at the Chumachenko table.

When the big shot's lawyer excused himself, Raven moved. He ignored Nadiya's protest and Petro's attempt to grab his arm. He let Tracy deal with their surprise.

Raven dropped into the empty chair. Chumachenko, in the middle of saying something to his accountant, stopped talking. The big shot's wife stared at him. Raven ignored her. He waited while Chumachenko met his eyes.

"Hello, Mr. Raven."

"No more pretense, huh? How long were your babysitters over there going to string us along?"

"Not much longer. You may even reach the climax of our little dance tonight."

"Where's Aaron Osborne?"

Chumachenko shrugged. "I have no idea."

"Your gimmick is going to cost thousands of lives. Is it worth it?"

"Ask my wife. Ask her daughters. There is a cancer in Crimea, Mr. Raven. It must be cut out."

"And help your tourist business?"

"There are benefits, yes. But if my government refuses to take action, we must, how do you Americans put it, light a fire behind their back?"

"Under their ass, actually."

"Much better expression."

Raven glanced at Vikka Chumachenko as she sipped a glass of wine. She apparently knew everything and didn't object. Ditto the accountant, who didn't look shocked or ask his boss what Raven's strange words meant.

The big shot surrounded himself with those who not only supported him, but worked to fulfill the goal.

There was a cancer in Crimea, all right. And it had nothing to do with the Nationalists. It had nothing to do with the Russian soldiers in the streets. The cancer sat inches from Raven. If they hadn't been in public, he'd have taken steps to wipe out the group where they sat.

The lawyer returned from the toilet and spoke in protest to Chumachenko at the sight of Raven in his seat. Chumachenko calmed the stocky man with a raised hand. He said to Raven, "It's been a pleasure to see your face after hearing so many things. I trust our next visit will be our last."

"You can count on it," Raven said. "And I don't like your odds."

"I promise your chance of survival is equally as low as mine. I look forward to seeing who comes out on top."

Raven didn't say goodnight. He left the table with a grim look, and shared the look with Nadiya and Petro when he returned to his table. He said to Nadiya, "I understand you have something for us?"

"We've received no orders."

"Okay." To Tracy, "We go back to the hotel and wait for these Mouseketeers to get their act together."

"Let's play gin again," Tracy suggested. "I can go on beating you all night."

Raven didn't respond. He glanced back at Chumachenko and realized he'd rattled the big shot more than he knew. Chumachenko had turned his body to look over his shoulder at Raven and stare. Raven picked up his water glass and raised it in a toast.

Not long until they settled accounts.

His phone beeped. He looked at the screen. A text from Aaron.

This needs to end. I made a mistake. Let's talk.

Raven: *Where are you.*

Aaron texted back an address. "Here we go," Raven said. "Nadiya, I'm going to need your car."

"No."

"Look under the table, Nadiya."

She did, but her face remained stoic. He held the Browning dead-center with her crotch. It would be an ugly shot. Petro didn't have to look to know Tracy had him covered as well.

Raven said, "We're going to leave without making a fuss or causing a scene. Let your boss pick up the check. Once we are outside, you will hand us the keys to your car and Tracy and me will investigate this obvious trap you've set. Unless it's not. In which case, tell your boss his number's up. The prodigal son is coming home. Again."

_____

THIRTY MINUTES EARLIER:

"Where are we going?" Aaron said. They had returned to

Kerch but were driving through an area of small family homes. Aaron noticed the spaces between the houses grew further apart the longer they drove. Untended and overgrown greenery filled the gaps, and the houses showed a mix of care and neglect. Not every home had a car parked out front.

Draco said, "The safe house. We'll stay here tonight. Second set of tasks tomorrow morning."

"What's wrong with where we've been staying?"

"Boss's orders."

"Right."

Draco continued driving. The forest grew thicker. Less houses now.

"Draco—"

The Ukrainian mercenary moved his right hand in a flash. He jammed the muzzle of his pistol into Aaron's midsection and pulled the trigger. The unsuppressed explosion filled the car and hurt Draco's ears. It was worse for Aaron Osborne. He not only screamed, but clawed for Raven's gun. Draco fired again. Aaron slumped against the passenger door. Raven's .45 tumbled onto the floor at his feet.

Finally. The dumb son of a bitch was dead. Draco jammed the hot pistol back under his left arm.

He turned into the driveway of a single-level cottage with thick brush and trees on both sides. The front yard was a mass of overgrowth and dirt. The driveway pavement had a large crack on one side where the slab had raised above the lawn.

Draco shifted into park and jumped from the cab. The front door opened and two men came out to meet him.

"Passenger side," Draco said. He stood back while the two men lifted Aaron Osborne out and carried him between them. They went back into the house. Draco grabbed the

Nighthawk Custom .45 ACP, locked the truck, and entered the house. He shut the door behind him.

The two men dropped Aaron's body on a bed in a back room. Draco ignored the messy interior as he headed down the hallway. The pair waited for him. Draco picked up Aaron's cell phone.

"You two armed?"

"Side arms and submachine guns," one said.

"We'll have company soon. Get ready."

The two men left the room. Draco looked at Aaron's body. His wounds dripped blood onto the already stained carpet, so no damage done. He didn't think the new stains would hurt. Draco shook his head. Aaron might have been a good man to have on his side. The man who proposed their entire scheme and put it in motion. The man who wanted to bring about Draco's dream of killing more Russians and make a little money on the side. Instead, he'd been weak and sentimental. He never should have included friends or a girl-friend in the mission.

Draco examined the cell phone. He scrolled through Aaron's contact list until he found Raven's number.

He sent a text pretending to be Aaron.

Only a matter of time before the man with the hero complex showed up. Then their problems would no longer exist.

43

THE RUSSIANS WORKING TO SOLVE THE CASE MADE PROGRESS without any help from the Americans.

The city-sweep of Nationalist suspects produced information leading to arms caches in Kerch. They found nothing in connection with a false flag attack.

It was Watcher One and Watcher Two, arrested while trying to kill Sam Raven, who broke under interrogation and gave the needed answers. Once they spilled, the Russians put the pieces together.

The two suspects named Osborne and one mentioned Chumachenko. The statement shocked the Kremlin when the Russian president demanded an update. But he refused to make a move until they learned more.

The Russian president had the luxury of time. Watcher One and Two said their compatriots were assembling a truck bomb to blow up the Crimean Bridge. The plan was for somebody to drive out to the center of the span and detonate the bomb. Russian FSB agents took up surveillance on an auto repair shop in Kerch the suspects talked about. On the day Draco drove his convoy to the militia, another truck entered the garage. It did not come out. The FSB planned to raid the shop and arrest everybody inside. If they confirmed the Chumachenko connection, the Russian president promised no hesitation. He'd bring the mogul back to Moscow for a private chat.

THE GPS SAID: "Turn left in 500 feet."

They'd changed the language to English.

Raven followed the directions. Tracy rode beside him, though every time he glanced at her, she was scanning for danger.

Nadiya and Petro had done as ordered under the nose of the big boss. Raven wished he could relish the subterfuge but was instead too focused on Aaron's message.

Had he decided to flip? Had his message prevented whatever plan Chumachenko had mentioned at the table?

"Take it easy," Tracy said.

"I'm fine."

"I mean slow down."

Raven let off the accelerator. The houses grew further and further apart, and the forest thicker. Raven became cautious.

"This might be an ambush," he said.

"Look there. House on the left."

"Behind those trees?"

GPS: "Your destination is on the left."

"Correct," Tracy said.

Raven slowed some more. If any shooting started, he was ready to mash the gas. The car drifted past the cottage. Truck in front, lights on within.

Tracy kept her eyes on the house. She took off her seat belt to turn for a better look.

"Clear in front. Recognize that truck?"

"Yeah," Raven said.

He pressed the gas. He drove another mile, the forest thicker with no homes now, until he found a place to turn around. He stopped on the side of the road and grabbed his phone.

"What are you doing, Raven?"

"I want to hear Aaron's voice." He dialed, listened, frowned.

"Hi, this is Aaron..."

Raven killed the connected and texted **Pick up, dammit**. He waited. No response. He called again. Voicemail. He put the phone away.

"It's a trap."

Raven pressed his lips together and banged a fist on the door.

Either Aaron was trying to lead him and Tracy to their deaths, or...

The *or* bothered him most.

"What do you want to do?" Tracy asked.

Raven tapped a finger on the steering wheel. What to do indeed.

How many in the house?

Was Aaron inside?

If so, was he being used as bait to bring in Raven and Tracy?

If so, when the enemy sprung the trap, would he change sides?

Aaron couldn't bring himself to kill Raven before. He had the chance in Sparks before the FBI showed up. What changed?

"Raven?"

"What?"

"We have to go in there."

He nodded. "We approach on foot, separate directions, and improvise."

"Okay."

"I'll go first and cut around back. Give me two minutes."

He opened the door and stepped out into the night.

DRACO EXPECTED the call and ignored both the ring and the text message.

His two associates, whom he'd christened Shooter One and Shooter Two because he couldn't be bothered to note the names of cannon fodder, yelled to him that the car had driven out of sight.

Draco ordered Shooter Two out the back. He told him to open fire on Raven and the woman when he saw them. Shooter Two moved fast through the kitchen to the back door.

Draco checked the submachine gun they'd provided. The CZ Scorpion EVO 3 was a good weapon and he had the fire selector set to full auto.

On his knees on the worn carpet, he peeked through a curtain. He tried to discern movement in the darkness beyond, but it wasn't possible. He might as well have been staring into the void of deep space.

Anything might be out there.

Raven might have called a battalion of US Marines. Draco and his shooters with their SMGs and pistols would be no match.

Preposterous.

Only Raven and the woman were out there. Only Raven and the woman. No Marines, no FSB. They had nobody to help them.

The final battle would begin soon. Once the war began

anew, Draco would have his chance for revenge against the Russian war machine.

Come on, Raven.

I have a war to finish.

———

RAVEN DROPPED flat in the hard-packed dirt. Dried chunks broke apart beneath him. Whoever left the cottage through the back door didn't shut it the right way. He made too much noise.

He held the Browning at the ready and wished for a suppressor, and sub-sonic ammo. But it wasn't Christmas yet; he couldn't ask Santa for any favors.

The shooter blended with the cluster of trees on the side of the cottage. The trees concealed part of the back patio. One of the tree branches moved. Raven aimed. He fired four shots in a square pattern, and held back on a fifth. Three of the shots missed but one scored. The shooter screamed. Raven fired again. He jumped up and ran as the shooter fell sideways. His body was visible under the branches, and Raven fired twice more to keep him on the ground for good. He stowed the Hi-Power and grabbed the man's EVO 3. A quick pat down and he found two spare magazines which he stuffed in the left pocket of his jacket.

Raven stepped onto the patio. Rusted metal chairs and a dirty table provided little cover, but he took advantage. He crouched behind the table and waited a moment. When nobody came through the door he rose, approached the door, and flung it open. He stepped aside to avoid exposure. He fired a burst inside, then bent low and ran into the cottage.

In the dark he made it only two steps before colliding with the edge of the island in the center of the kitchen. He hit the floor and gunfire blazed through the doorway to the next room. Raven slid across the floor to the other side of the island. He peeked around but didn't see the shooter.

Raven moved diagonally to the right of the doorframe, covering the opening at an angle. He fired. Shifting to cover the left side, he fired again. Somebody panicked. A gunman ran down the hall from the left side of the doorway. Raven ran through, firing, pivoting to cover his backside. No other threats. Raven slapped a full magazine into the EVO and leaned against the wall.

"Aaron!"

No response.

Raven cursed. Glass shattered up front. An SMG crackled. Raven moved ahead. Two pistol shots popped and another full-auto burst joined the commotion.

Tracy screamed.

Raven ran.

44

THE SHOOTING AT THE REAR OF THE COTTAGE GAVE TRACY THE edge she needed.

One light burned inside, glowing behind the curtained windows. When the shooting started, she watched a shadow move against the light. Running to the side of the road, she found a rock. More gunfire popped within. She flung the rock at the front window. Glass shattered. She ran to the door and blasted the lock, jumping to one side. A burst of return fire came her way. Swinging low through the doorway, she brought up her pistol and scanned for targets.

The first was easy. A gunman came running down the hall into the front room. Tracy stopped him with two shots to the chest and a third to the head before he fell.

She pivoted right as a second man with an SMG rose from behind a chair. She fired once and missed. She dived out of the way as he fired back. Tracy rolled as the shots landed somewhere behind her and bumped into a table. A lamp tumbled onto her back. She let out a startled scream, then fired a string of shots in the gunner's direction as he moved.

Another figure appeared in the hallway. She swung her gun over but held back as she recognized Raven.

"On your left!" she shouted.

RAVEN BROUGHT up the Scorpion as Draco swung his weapon at his midsection. Raven fired first. The salvo opened Draco stomach to chest. He froze, a look of pain flooding his face for a short moment, then fell. Raven ran to him and kicked the SMG across the floor.

He ran to Tracy. "You okay?"

She stood. "Yeah."

Raven headed for the hallway again. "Aaron!"

Tracy joined him as he began checking rooms, calling out Osborne's name each time. When he reached the back bedroom, he didn't say anything. He froze in the doorway with his eyes on his friend's dead body.

Raven stepped into the room and felt his friend's face. He was almost cold. Raven thumbed Aaron's eyes closed.

"Raven?"

"This is not what I wanted."

"What did you want?"

"A last chance to talk some sense into him."

She pulled on his shirt. "We gotta go."

Raven sighed. "Yeah. There's nothing more to do here."

They left the room for the front but Raven stopped to check Draco's body. He found Aaron's phone. The text was now explained. A further search turned up his Nighthawk Custom Talon .45 ACP. He checked the gun and put it in his belt.

"Grab the sub guns and magazines," he said. "We'll need them. And let's take the truck out front."

Tracy began gathering guns. "Why?"

"They used it this morning and somebody might recognize it when we visit Chumachenko."

They ran out. Two steps off the porch another car approached. Raven and Tracy ran for cover as the car stopped short in the driveway, blocking the truck's exit. Two people piled out. Nadiya and Petro had arrived to check the carnage but now they'd join the corpses.

Tracy fired first, catching Petro in the neck. He fell against the car and tumbled to the ground. Nadiya moved faster, firing for effect as she ran to the rear bumper.

"Keep her occupied," Raven told Tracy. He broke left, jumping off the porch. Nadiya winged a shot his way. Tracy fired back. He ran in a wide circle and then headed for the car. Nadiya swung her gun to Tracy but her return fire nicked a tree. Raven took a shot and punctured the rear fender, missing the tire. Nadiya pulled back. Raven closed the distance at a sprint, stopping short. When she appeared again, he was in front of her. The flash of fire from the muzzle of the EVO 3 turned one side of her face bright red mush mixed with bone. Her body flopped. He shot her again for good measure.

Petro moaned.

Raven stepped over to the mousy man and used one more bullet to put him out of his misery.

Tracy ran over. "Maybe we should take their car."

"Help me move the bodies."

She did.

They were on the road when Wilson called Tracy's cell. She answered and put the CIA man on speaker.

"Where are you?" Wilson said.

Raven gave the update.

"All right, listen up. Things have changed and the Russians have a request..."

CHUMACHENKO PACED HIS HOME OFFICE.

He'd heard nothing from Draco. Nadiya and Petro had also failed to report. He'd given them ample time to do so. It meant only one thing. Raven and Tracy had survived and were now coming for him.

"Orest?"

He stopped in mid step and turned. Vikka stood in the doorway wrapped in a long coat and holding a suitcase.

"I'm ready," she said.

He was already packed. All he needed was the briefcase sitting on his desk. The case contained a laptop and other necessary documents. "We shall leave immediately," he told her. He went to his desk, grabbed the case with one hand and the phone with the other. He ordered the car brought around front. Chumachenko joined his wife, took her suitcase in his free hand, and they hurried down the hall. They passed mounted paintings and sculptures which had brought them so much joy for so long. They didn't give them a second glance.

Only survival mattered now. The plan was still going forward; nothing could stop it. But they had to survive the two Americans if they were to see the glory of their effort come to pass.

Sam Raven was proving a worthy adversary. Chumachenko wished their involvement had been one of allies rather than antagonists.

The black Mercedes waited at the top of the circular driveway at the foot of the porch steps. Two guards would travel with them—driver and front passenger. Each were discreetly armed with Glock machine pistols. What remained of his modest support crew would stay behind.

Chumachenko loaded Vikka's suitcase with his already in

the trunk. He kept his briefcase with him on his lap. The driver departed, following the curving driveway to the left. He straightened for the short run to the gate, now open, and the road beyond.

The headlamps shined brightly, catching the immaculate lawn in the wide beams. Chumachenko had been proud of his lawn, though he'd never lifted a finger to care for it. He let his garden crew handle the chores. He'd see the lawn again, soon, once the problems were over and the plan in full operation.

He took Vikka's hand and squeezed. Her return smile was weak. Her hand felt cold. The Mercedes slowed to pass through the gate and turn right. The tires bit into the pavement and the Mercedes surged ahead with a blast of horsepower.

The road curved, and another car came toward them. Chumachenko let go of Vikka's hand. He started to speak to the driver but choked as the oncoming car veered into the path of the Mercedes.

Vikka screamed. The driver stomped the brakes and activated the emergency brake. The car spun in a bootlegger's 180-degree turn. Rubber burned as the tires screeched on the pavement. The Mercedes stopped with the front end pointed in the direction they'd come from. Brake off, pedal down; too late. *Impact*.

45

THE REAR COLLISION JOLTED THE MERCEDES. CHUMACHENKO and his wife lurched forward. The Mercedes, still in motion as the other car hit, fishtailed, and the other car didn't stop. The front bumper ground into the Mercedes as it spun, forcing a violent spin out. The rear wheels left the pavement and the car jolted again as they dug into the shoulder. The Mercedes stopped half off the road. The other car halted at an angle, blocking the Mercedes from going forward.

Chumachenko's heart beat in his throat. Vikka hyperventilated beside him. He kept an arm around her and yelled for the guards to get out and shoot. He didn't have to ask twice. They sprang from the car with machine pistols in hand. Chumachenko pressed his still-screaming wife to the floor and covered her with his body. The shooting began.

Tracy slid out of the car and onto the pavement. Raven crawled across the seat to join her.

Rapid machine pistol fire smacked into the car. Metal ripped and glass popped. Tracy fired her Scorpion around the bumper. Raven ran to the rear and added several bursts to the fray. Both shooters toppled as bullets tore through their chests and left red chunks of flesh splattered on the ground.

Raven dropped the Scorpion and took out his .45. The checkered wooden grips felt good in his hand.

"Cover me!"

He didn't wait for Tracy's reply. Raven moved forward to skirt the front of the Mercedes. Two people in back. A man and a woman. The man raised his head. Raven grinned at the terrified face of Orest Chumachenko.

"Get out of the car!"

Chumachenko spoke to his wife. She looked up. Tears blotted her cheeks. She argued and grabbed her husband as he opened the back door. He brushed her hand away. Chumachenko stepped out and straightened his coat.

"I admire you, Mr. Raven. You're a hard man to kill."

"Raise your hands."

Chumachenko complied. "I am unarmed. Not even you would shoot a man with no weapon."

"Are you sure? I've done it quite a bit, Orest."

Doubt flickered across the big shot's face, but he recovered and took a deep breath. He resumed his business face. "What do we do now?"

"I'm turning you and your wife over to the Russians."

"You think doing so will make them forget about the murders you have committed on their soil? You aren't walking away from here, Mr. Raven. There will be consequences."

Chumachenko's eyes flashed down. Then back to Raven. Raven pretended not to notice. The passenger-seat guard lay bleeding between them. His machine pistol was within reach if Chumachenko moved fast enough.

"The joke is on you, Orest. We had a chat with the CIA on the way over. The Russians have raided the auto shop where you were building your truck bomb. There will be no war. Not the way you intended, anyway."

"What—"

"It's over," Raven said. "Your buddies in the Kremlin have a few things to talk over with you. My partner and I get a free pass for handing you over."

"You're lying."

"Am I?"

Chumachenko blinked.

Raven said, "How else would I know about the auto shop? Draco was too dead to talk."

"I'll surrender," Chumachenko said, "if you leave my wife out of this."

"Why?"

"Tell them your investigation showed she had no knowledge, Mr. Raven, that is all."

"You haven't told me why, Orest."

"Because this wasn't *only* about *me*."

"You killed my friend. And you killed his father. I'm not granting any favors."

"My briefcase is in the car. Turn me and the case over to the Russians and they will have everything. Leave my wife alone."

"They'll get the case anyway, Orest."

"I'll give you the code to turn off the explosive pack."

"It's rigged?"

"Open it wrong and yes, the bomb within will be devastating. Do what I ask and you will have the code."

"No. I'll tell them it's rigged and they can defuse it. Who do you think you're playing with, Orest?"

Tracy said, "Raven."

"What?"

"I hear them."

Approaching sirens. They registered with Raven too.

And Chumachenko made his move.

He dived for the machine pistol. His wife screamed. Chumachenko wrapped his hand around the gun, brought up the muzzle—

The .45 in Raven's hand roared once. Chumachenko's head snapped back and he dropped flat. His wife kept screaming. She tumbled out of the car and grasped at his body with her face in his neck.

Raven turned around. A black sedan with flashing cherry lights, its siren screaming, approached. A troop truck full of Russian soldiers drove behind the sedan. The beams of their headlamps highlighted the wreck. Raven raised an arm to block the glare. He stood by Tracy as the vehicles stopped. The sirens cut off. Troops jumped from the truck. Four FSB officers exited the sedan. Raven and Tracy set their weapons down.

Vikka Chumachenko's anguished cries drowned out any other sound. Her screaming matched those of so many others sacrificed in the name of the war business.

46

"THE INFORMATION CHUMACHENKO HAD ON HIS LAPTOP
answered a lot of questions."

"The biggest one being," Raven said, "how the heck did he
and Osborne get together?"

"And?"

"And when did Aaron and his father have their actual
reunion?"

They sat in a small conference room at CIA headquarters.
Raven and Tracy had returned to the United States less than
24 hours earlier, and the whirlwind trip from Ukraine and
rush into debrief left Raven dizzy. He didn't know how Tracy
felt, but guessed the same. She sat quietly at the table next to
Raven. Clark Wilson sat across from them with his laptop.
Wilson consulted notes as they spoke.

"From what Chumachenko recorded, the idea was
hatched between Aaron and Draco while they worked on an
oil rig in the Mediterranean."

"Makes sense," Raven said.

"Aaron brought it to his father six months ago. We don't
know how they reconnected; Chumachenko didn't note the

details, but Mark Osborne knew Chumachenko from previous deals. It was Mark who approached *him*."

Tracy said, "How did they know each other?"

"Apparently Mr. Osborne has been dealing from the bottom of the deck a long time, but avoiding detection. Chumachenko made notes about everything. They've made numerous illegal arms deals together. We know who they've dealt with, how, and when. It was probably his insurance policy in case anybody pulled a fast one."

"Bad guys always write stuff down," Raven said.

"Osborne and Chumachenko had a few meetings, negotiated what either side would do, and put Aaron and Draco in charge of the rest."

"Ripping off the plant would have gone well," Tracy said, "if we hadn't been around."

"You two were never supposed to make it out of France alive. Chumachenko's notes say he was very upset Aaron kept you around."

"He couldn't do it," Raven said. "He could con us into helping, but couldn't bring himself to tie off loose ends."

"His Achilles heel," Wilson said.

"Why didn't Draco's mercs pull off the Dacourt robbery?" Raven said.

"They were too busy infiltrating into the country for the hit on the plant," Wilson said. "We have the routes and contacts they used to sneak in. We'll plug those holes soon enough, believe me. Right now, the DCI has decided to watch the smugglers for a bit and see who else they bring in."

"Playing with fire, Clark," Raven said. "Close down the pipelines before they slip somebody in really dangerous."

"Talks are ongoing," Wilson said. "You're not the only one in the building with that opinion, although you are the only non-employee saying so." He smiled.

Raven smiled back. His green "guest" badge only allowed

access to certain areas of the building, and not without an escort.

"What's next?" Raven said.

"Osborne Defense is under official investigation, and thereby all business and manufacturing has been halted," Wilson said. "When the Feds are done the board of directors will likely shut everything down and dissolve the company. Aaron was an only child. No heirs to take over."

"They probably wouldn't want to anyway," Tracy said, "after what's happened."

"We closed down a major arms pipeline and stopped a war," Wilson said. "I think that's enough for today, don't you?"

"There's always next time," Raven said. "And maybe we won't be fast enough to stop it."

Wilson closed the laptop. "You're always a waterfall of optimism, Sam."

"Been around too long."

"When does your plane leave for Stockholm?"

"Three hours."

"Enjoy the jet lag. You've been coming and going so much your body is going to need a week to catch up."

Raven forced a smile. He wanted to say he was used to it, and maybe he was, and it was all the excuse he needed to take a long vacation.

Until the ghosts called him again.

The meeting ended with quiet sighs all around. They were exhausted from the fight and its personal toll. Raven only wanted to get home to Stockholm and his house boat and take a long break. Wilson escorted them out of the building where he and Raven said goodbye, and Tracy led him to her car.

She drove him to Dulles. Traffic turned the thirty-minute drive into a forty-five-minute journey, but neither spoke.

Every time he glanced at her to say something, the tightness of her jaw and grip on the wheel dissuaded him. She didn't want to talk. She knew Raven was going to bring up her father, so he kept his mouth shut. He didn't even bother to make a crack about the traffic.

But when he saw the Dulles Airport Pond on his right, he knew they were getting closer to the terminal. If he didn't speak now, they'd probably never speak again.

"I was serious about helping you," he said.

She slowed for traffic heading to the departure building. Her shoulders sank a little, her face softened. She looked like she was about to cry. "I know," she said.

"If your father is out there, we can find him. Or we can find out what happened. You deserve to know."

"I'll keep it in mind," she said. "Part of me doesn't want to know. Part of me wants to think he's still alive and doing his job."

"But the other part—"

"Knows he's gone."

Raven pressed his lips together. He said nothing more. Tracy pulled up at the departure terminal and stopped the car. More traffic passed by on the left. The sidewalk to the right was already crowded with travelers, luggage, and airport attendants. Airport police directed traffic and blew whistles. Everyday airport chaos, and nobody knew, or cared, about the private drama playing out in one of the cars.

Raven left the front seat to collect his carry-on and suitcase from the back. He shut the door. She powered down the passenger window as he leaned in to say goodbye.

"Call me when you're ready," he said.

"Yeah." She smiled. "Thanks for everything. Sam."

Raven smiled back, waved, and turned away. He couldn't force her to do what she wasn't ready to do, but at least he'd cracked the ice. She'd finally called him by his first name. As he reached the automatic doors, he looked back. She had already blended into the line of traffic and was gone.

He entered the terminal to check in for his flight.

The jet took off after a twenty-minute delay and Raven sat alone in first class. He absently flipped through the in-flight magazine with the shade pulled down over his window. He didn't need to see Washington fall away as the plane climbed into the sky. He'd seen the place enough.

The experience with Aaron had been rough. It was not going to be an easy recovery. Betrayal was like death—you never got over it. And in this case, his friend also died. Raven had hoped one final confrontation with Aaron might turn him around. But Chumachenko had stolen the opportunity from him, and he'd never know if he might have saved Aaron's life the way Aaron had once saved his.

He regretted not being able to do more. Aaron had been a victim of his own greed, probably passed down from his father, but there had been some good left in him. Otherwise, he'd have killed Raven without hesitating.

He'd carry the pain with him, as he always did, and learn to live with the ghosts. He couldn't save everybody, but he'd never stop trying to save the ones he could as he followed their call around the world. The war without end was living up to its name.

And then there was Tracy. Lost in her own world of uncertainty, convinced remaining in the shadows was the way to find out what happened to her father. She was right, he was probably gone. Only a vengeance mission lay ahead. But it was easy for Raven to suggest they get on with it. For her to admit her father was gone meant a final goodbye she wasn't ready for. Raven touched the locket under his shirt. He'd had his share of unwanted goodbyes, too. It was better to pretend there was still a chance her father would show up at her door one day with an explanation. She needed the hope more than the truth. For now.

Maybe someday she'd realize she needed permanent closure. Raven would be there to help. Because somebody had to play hero and help those unable to help themselves. Even fighters like Tracy needed a champion.

He wondered where his ghosts would send him next. All he knew for sure was the next time was coming soon, because monsters lurked in the shadows, and he needed to find them. But now, for a moment, he could rest.

ABOUT THE AUTHOR

A twenty-five year veteran of radio and television broadcasting, Brian Drake has spent his career in San Francisco where he's filled writing, producing, and reporting duties with stations such as KPIX-TV, KCBS, KQED, among many others. Currently carrying out sports and traffic reporting duties for Bloomberg 960, Brian Drake spends time between reports and carefully guarded morning and evening hours cranking out action/adventure tales.

A love of reading when he was younger inspired him to create his own stories, and he sold his first short story, "The Desperate Minutes," to an obscure webzine when he was 25 (more years ago than he cares to remember, so don't ask).

Brian Drake lives in California with his wife and two cats, and when he's not writing he is usually blasting along the back roads in his Corvette with his wife telling him not to drive so fast, but the engine is so loud he usually can't hear her.

briandrakebooks.com